DOUGLAS ... ...ɔ there and

a series of historical crime novels ... .
...cotland featuring investigative advocate John MacKenzie and
...is side-kick Davie Scougall. He is also the author of *The Price of*
...otland, a prize-winning history of Scotland's Darien Disaster.
...e lives in Midlothian with his wife Julie.

...tt conjures up a convincingly dark atmosphere on this cusp
...he age of reason.
...E HERALD on *Testament of a Witch*

...ue over Rebus. There's a new – or should that be old – detective
...wn.
... EDINBURGH on *Death of a Chief*

...uthor vividly brings to life late 17th century Edinburgh
...NAL OF THE LAW SOCIETY OF SCOTLAND on *Death of a Chief*

...tionally well written, it reads like a novel. As I say – if
...e not Scottish and live here – read it. If you're Scottish
...t anyway. It's a very, very good book.
...EDINBURGH on *The Price of Scotland*

...las Watt has brought an economist's eye and poet's sen-
...y in The Price of Scotland... *to show definitively... that*
...ambition and mismanagement, rather than English men-
...doomed Scotland's imperial ambitions.

...BSERVER on *The Price of Scotland*

...st-have book on the events in advance of the Act of Union
...ught Scotland and England together in 1707 is Douglas
Watt's *The Price of Scotland. It's a fantastic run-through of the*
'catastrophic failure' of the Darien Scheme – the creation of the
Company of Scotland to establish a Central American colony.
FINANCIAL TIMES on *The Price of Scotland*

The Unnatural Death of a Jacobite

DOUGLAS WATT

Luath Press Limited

EDINBURGH

www.luath.co.uk

First published 2019

ISBN: 978-1-912147-61-8

The author's right to be identified as author of this book under
the Copyright, Designs and Patents Act 1988 has been asserted.

The paper used in this book is recyclable. It is made from low
chlorine pulps produced in a low energy, low emission manner
from renewable forests.

Printed and bound by Bell & Bain Ltd., Glasgow

Typeset in 10.5 point Sabon by Lapiz

To Katie

Acknowledgements

THANKS TO MY WIFE Julie for all her love and support, and to everyone at Luath Press.

List of Main Characters

John MacKenzie – advocate

Aeneas MacLeod – lawyer

Elizabeth MacKenzie – daughter of John MacKenzie

Kenneth MacKenzie, Earl of Seaforth – chief of Clan MacKenzie

Ruairidh MacKenzie – brother of Seaforth

Davie Scougall – notary public, MacKenzie's assistant

Archibald Stirling – ex Crown Officer, friend of MacKenzie

Mary Erskine, Mrs Hair – moneylender

David Drummond – Jacobite lawyer

Betty McGrain – office girl

William Galbraith – writer

Adam Scobie – Presbyterian writer

George Gourlay – Edinburgh tavern owner

John Dalrymple, Master of Stair – Lord Advocate

Andrew Stein – Captain of the Town Guard

Patrick Cranstoun, Earl of Dewarton – nobleman

Prologue

THE HALBERD IS A DIFFICULT weapon to use in combat. You need real strength in your arms to wield it. Without enough power in your shoulders you cannot direct it down at the correct angle and move it swiftly enough to kill your enemy. You'd be cleaved in two yourself before you'd have time to use it. Some say it's an old-fashioned weapon, a slow and ponderous one. It's not the weapon of choice of the soldier of today. Other weapons have replaced it, smaller, lighter and more efficient ones. But this is not a battlefield. There is no Papist enemy rushing towards you screaming in blood lust. No deafening explosions of artillery surround you. There is no blind confusion and deafening roars. None of the panic of battle, none of the fear, no desperate cries. There is none of the shit and piss and rambling confessions of men and boys before the attack. No last testaments scribbled by those who can write, preparing to find themselves, perhaps in the next minute or second, in Heaven or Hell, or some other place.

This is not a battlefield. This is a chamber under the city of Edinburgh in the kingdom of Scotland. To wield such a long weapon in a confined space feels wrong. It feels like there is not enough room to swing it properly, despite the vaulted ceiling being a good twenty feet above your head; it's still constrictive. You must be careful not to strike the roof and upset the weapon's motion. At least there is no need to judge the distance of the charge. You can take your time down here. You have all the time in the world. The enemy is not a cavalry man bearing down on you, or an infantryman with raised sword preparing to slash you. The enemy is strapped to a wooden chair a few feet in front of you. The enemy is bound and gagged. He cannot curse you or spit on you. But you can see terror in his eyes.

You have dragged him from the streets above. A few minutes ago, he was sharing a cup of ale with cronies in a tavern. He was laughing at lewd jokes, discussing a political point or boasting about the conquest of a lass, while he munched on a pie. Disbelief is evident in his eyes. He has no idea what this is all about. He does not know who has ordered his removal from the world above and demanded his presence in the one beneath. He is unable to take in what is happening to him; his sudden descent into the underworld to be faced with a beast, a monster from his nightmares. A monster wielding a halberd. That is the way it must be in this place. The hair mask, the great horns on the helmet, the furs over your shoulders, transforming you into a monster from the world of nightmares. You can smell the piss on his breeks now. The urine pools and steams on the stone floor around the chair. Even the bravest man is brought low by closeness to death. No, it is not your weapon of choice. But it is a weapon of theatre. For in this battle, theatre is everything. You have learned that. You must put on a good show. The other one, the younger one held in the corner, is also gagged. He is a witness to the gore. He will return to the world above. He will spread a story about a monster beneath the city. Most will not believe him, but a few will wonder. A dagger to rip the throat or a sword to open the chest would make more sense. It would be much quicker and easier, but where is the theatre in that?

Do you feel any sympathy for the creature in front of you? Does he have a wife and children? Is he a good man or a bad one? Should he be punished for his sins or was he a saint who should be praised? You know nothing about him. You do not want to know. But if you do not act you will find yourself like this poor creature, despite your experience of killing.

You have waited long enough in the damp chamber. You stand for a few moments more, allowing them to take in the horror, letting them linger in silence. Behold a monster from the deep! It is so far below the city his screams will not be heard above. They will echo through the subterranean labyrinth of this other world, a world dug out over hundreds, perhaps thousands of years, a world you now claim as your own. For few others can claim it. Few others possess the fury to claim it as you have. You stand in a chamber of death under the foundations of churches and manses, where ministers preach and elders pontificate. This is another world in which the kirk session has no power. Here the nobles hold no sway, the King is an ordinary mortal and all the generals in the army are powerless. You are lord in this subterranean country. In this land, you are King.

You can smell his shit now. The creature knows he is about to die. He realises his last moments will be ones of unimaginable horror. The end which you are about to bring to fruition is more disturbing than any death on the battlefield, where a soldier is taken by blade, bullet or shrapnel. At least in battle you die with honour and you leave that honour behind for your family. But this is a time of peace, or at least relative peace. The city is quiet for now, folk above are going about their business; writers writing instruments, merchants making deals, fleshers slashing meat, coopers building barrels. And here you perform your business. The business of killing. It's a profession few can pursue. You cannot change your work now. You have chosen this path, the route of slaughter. You have chosen the life of gore. There is only one law in this world, in this Hades, in this Hell. You must kill or be killed. You must do everything to survive. It is the simple rule you have followed since you were a boy – all politics and religion and universities and schools are nothing compared to this brutal law which has governed your life since you were left an orphan, starving and alone, but hungry to survive.

It is time to end it. You are godlike in this moment. Whether to wait a minute longer, ten minutes, an hour, suspend time, extend life, prolong the horror of his last pitiful moments. Let him speak a few words, allow him to scream and beg, give him time for a last prayer, one final confession of his sins, perhaps. But not this time. You are tired of waiting. You swing the weapon. You remember the feel of it on the battlefield. The tip of the halberd is only a few feet from the vaulted ceiling at its apex. You are not a creature entirely without sentiment, without some shred of morality. For some dark creatures would have teased him, tempted him with hope, prolonged the agony. They might have tortured him for one reason only – that they were able to do so. But you are not like them. You have a slither of humanity in your black soul. You want to get it done, now. The blade whistles through the air. The blade slices down, thunderously. The blade cleaves straight through him as if he is not there. No need for much pressure, just the weight of the weapon in its arc through the fetid air and the sharpness of the blade. Clean through flesh and bone. An explosion of tissue. An attempt to scream through the gag for an instant. The shudder of death through the body. And it is done. Your work is done. Blood gushes onto the floor, a red burn in spate, surrounding the chair, spreading into a crimson flower. The man is gone to another place, the place some call Heaven and some call Hell, or that other place called Nothing, the place you believe in, despite the rantings of the men of God. The kingdom of mighty Nothing is where all creatures must resort after their days are done. Does it matter how or when you arrive in that place? Does it matter on which day you find yourself there? You do not think it does. The man's head drops forward as the life fluid seeps from severed vessels, ripped tissue and fractured bones. You always have the same thought when you watch the moment of death on the battlefield or in the slaughter house. One day it will be you. That day draws closer. That day is one day closer. You cannot escape mighty Nothing. It will have you soon enough. But until that day, you will fight it. You will fight with blood, until that day when you, like him, sit on the throne of death waiting for the halberd to fall.

CHAPTER I

Golf on Musselburgh Links

IT WAS THE FIRST TIME they had all played together since MacKenzie and Scougall had returned from the Highlands two weeks before. MacKenzie stood on the first tee, deep in thought, staring north across the grey sheet of water to Fife beyond. The journey north to MacKenzie clan lands in Ross-shire searching for his daughter had been a complete failure. The trail for Elizabeth had run cold. They had searched back and forward across the Black Isle and round most of eastern Ross-shire from castle to castle and township to township for almost a month. They found nothing, only rumours of sightings a few weeks before, and rumours of rumours of sightings. Everyone was distracted by the war. The whole place was in a state of mayhem; the peace shattered when Dundee raised the standard for King James at Dundee Law. Another armed rising in the Highlands. They saw armed men everywhere and fear on every mother's face. The taste and smell of war. And God knew how long it would last. Once begun, civil war could last for years, even decades. It spread through the country until it dragged everything into its vortex. The last one had changed everything. It had changed the Highlands for good. It had changed the world, or so it had seemed. The world had been taken up in the hands of strife and thrown back down in another shape.

During the search, he had managed to keep his melancholy feelings at bay. He was focused entirely on finding her and Ruairidh MacKenzie, Seaforth's brother, whom she had eloped with. The thought that they were hiding out somewhere in MacKenzie lands was reasonable. A letter from his brother told him she had been seen at the house of MacKenzie of Kilcoy, but his brother had heard nothing more by the time they reached him. Elizabeth could have been anywhere by then – off to the west Highlands or as far away as the islands – Lewis was held by the MacKenzies – a much longer journey by boat across the Minch. Without definite intelligence of their whereabouts, it would be a wild goose chase. For all he knew, they could be with Dundee's army on its progress back and forth across the hills, in the game of cat and mouse with MacKay's forces. Ruairidh was, after all, a Papist and Jacobite. Dundee was seeking new recruits, making outlandish promises to the clans. It was even possible they had fled to King Louis's court in France or to Ireland where King James had gathered his forces and where Seaforth had escaped to. The thought of his duplicitous chief angered him and a wave of despair washed through him. The sinking of his spirits. A hatred of life. A desire for it all to end. The terrible thought kept returning, invading his mind. He might never see Elizabeth again. She was taken from him just as her mother had been over twenty years before. And he would be left alone.

Hatred of one's chief was a terrible emotion for a Highland man. It went against the grain. He should honour, obey and respect Seaforth, but Seaforth had lied to him and Ruairidh had tricked him. He would never forgive them. The fibres of his kinship were frayed. All he could do was keep in touch with his contacts in the Highlands – he had many clients from all parts – surely one would hear something. In the meantime, he must keep busy to curtail the dark feelings which kept rising within him. He had time on his hands since losing his job as Clerk of the Session at the Revolution. All those associated with the old regime had been dropped like stones down a well. The new government had to be cleansed of the stain of association with the Papist King James. Even though MacKenzie was no Papist, by upbringing an Episcopalian Protestant, it did not matter to the government. They viewed Episcopalians as Papists in all but name. And so, for the first time in decades he had time on his hands. There was a paralysis of legal business across the country and the courts were all closed. He would never return to his work at the Session unless there was another change in the government, a counter-revolution. This would only happen if Dundee defeated MacKay in battle and James returned as King.

A troubling question kept coming back to him – was James worth fighting for? James had proved a disastrous King. There was no doubt of that. Even his followers thought him a fool. But whatever the fool had done, he was still the lawful King of Scotland. The Stuart blood line went back hundreds of years. That still counted for much, especially in the Highlands. The Presbyterians might have support in the Lowlands and among the Campbell clans of the south west Highlands and Presbyterian clans around Inverness, like Munros and Rosses, but there were many who despised the Dutch impostor William and especially, the re-emergence of the Campbells as a power to be reckoned with. James could count on all those who opposed the Campbells: MacDonalds, MacKenzies, Camerons and a host of others. If he had been younger, he might have joined Dundee's army. But there was too much to lose to make a commitment either way. He was too old, anyway, to be useful in the field. There were other things he could do to aid the Jacobite cause. If that is what he wanted to do. He was uncertain. The most sensible policy was to sit on the fence and wait the turn of events.

MacKenzie turned from the view of the firth to watch Scougall address his ball on the first tee. Scougall steadied himself and drove powerfully down the fairway. It was a fine shot, as straight as an arrow from a bow. A beautiful thing to behold – Davie Scougall's golf swing! There was nothing half-hearted about it! MacKenzie reflected how Scougall had proved an attentive companion in the Highlands, even attempting to learn a few words of Gaelic, and joining a hunt in the hills despite lacking any ability as a horseman. The image of Scougall perched on his brother's mare with a gun in his hand and a plaid over his shoulder brought a smile to MacKenzie's face. That went against the grain too – Davie Scougall in the tartan!

The government in Edinburgh was nervous. Suspected Jacobites were under surveillance. He was sure he was being watched himself. A man in the shadows in the vennel across from his apartments or sitting in the Royal Coffee House watching him. He would be suspected as Seaforth's kinsman. Many of his clients came from MacKenzie septs under suspicion. The MacKenzies were a Jacobite clan in the same way the Campbells were a Williamite one. He knew his letters were being opened. It was all a God-awful mess. King James was an imbecile – his policies had alienated most of his subjects. Never had a King thrown away so much so quickly. Even his unlucky father, Charles, had taken longer to upset the apple cart – twenty-five years on the throne before losing his head. James had taken just three years to unhinge the whole regime. But the Prince of Orange had upset the established order. He could not quite work out why it was so distasteful to have a Dutchman on the throne of Scotland. However much he tried to rationalise that it might be good for foreign trade, he could not support the new regime, especially the vipers who benefitted from the old King's fall – grasping politicians and the fanatic ministers, Presbyterians and Covenanters espousing the grim tenets of Calvin, who whipped up the people by smearing their enemies as Papist and pulling the strings of the mob. Did he support the use of force to overthrow the new government? Would he provide funds for the Jacobites? There were too many political issues to consider when he should be concentrating on finding Elizabeth. Loyalty to King James burned through his veins when drinking in the tavern. In the cold light of day, he was a Jacobite, a reluctant one, but a Jacobite nonetheless. He knew he would toast the return of James with all his heart.

Stirling was next to play. His old friend had time on his hands too. As Crown Officer in the old regime he had also been swept aside by the new one. Stirling bent over stiffly to place his ball on the tee. He did not look well. He was pale and pasty, worried and distracted. Retirement was not good for him, although he had looked forward to it. Stirling took a hasty practice swing. There was something agitated in his movement.

He addressed the ball and swung inelegantly, hooking it into the rough about fifty yards away. Stirling swore violently, cursing the game.

'You don't look well today, Archibald,' said MacKenzie, playfully, as he placed his own ball on the tee. 'The sea air may do you some good.'

'I don't play well either. I've been afflicted by a fever for a few days, John. I only recover slowly. I fear it may be something more serious... an ague. I have not felt like myself since retirement was forced upon me. Perhaps I should consult a physician.'

'Retirement does not suit you? I thought you looked forward to it?'

'It's not as congenial as I'd hoped. My health has not been good since the day I left office. Perhaps too much leisure is bad for me. I'm forced to spend hours on negotiations for Arabella's marriage. And if that were not enough, I must spend time in Margaret's company. I'm not well suited to that. She's always on at me to be doing something in the house or round the estate: mend a fence or repair a wall or plant trees in the field by the river or look to improving yields by planting peas instead of oats and other new-fangled ideas. In the past, I left my man in charge of all such business. Margaret will not let a man be. I begin to miss my old work as Crown Officer. I thought I'd never say that, John. What's worse, I've no time for historical work. I've barely spent an hour on my History since the day I left office. I was sure it would be finished by now. Instead, I spend all my time marching around the estate or with Dewarton's lawyers or on shopping trips to buy new clothes for Arabella. My money is disappearing like water down a drain. Perhaps, I suffer from a stone. I've a pain here in my side. It flares up. It will not go away, whatever I eat.' Stirling held his hand against his side and grimaced. 'I may have to consult that little shit, Lawtie.'

MacKenzie laughed, lowered his head over the ball and concentrated. He hit his shot confidently down the middle. The ball came to rest about fifty yards behind Scougall's, a good enough first effort. As they set off down the fairway, he remembered the post was due that afternoon. It might bring a letter from his brother. The thought lightened his mood. There might be some news of Elizabeth at last. He watched the clouds moving in the wind over Fife. Strips of blue appeared in the north. The sun burst through and poured light onto the course. He suddenly had the feeling he would see her again. He knew it in his heart. Nothing would stop him seeing her again. He was surprised and pleased to have such an uplifting thought. Golf was indeed good for the soul!

CHAPTER 2

A Summer Storm

THE DELUGE BEGAN late in the afternoon after the round of golf and continued through the evening and all the way through the night. Sheets of relentless rain swept down across the Lothians. The rain swelled the Water of Leith until it burst its banks at Canon Mills and Stock Bridge. It lashed the sash windows of the high tenements across the city. It gushed down the precipitous rock of the castle in rivulets and flooded the Nor Loch, so it was no longer a shallow, stinking marsh, but transformed into a dark sheet of water, a loch proper. It fell on the High Street and the vennels and closes and wynds which led off it, creating huge puddles and pools. It flooded basements and soaked the deep caverns and tunnels under the city.

Scougall looked down from his window in Mrs Baird's lodgings just off the High Street. He had never seen the like of it in his life, such a relentless downpour in the summer, it was like a winter storm. It was as if God was angry with the realm of Scotland, as if He sought to cleanse the nation, wash away the sins of its depraved inhabitants, of whom there were many. It was a city of sin, indeed. A city full of evil and sin. A realm cleaved unto sin. So much sin. So much evil. He had already seen too much in his young life. But there was also good to balance the bad, he reflected. Men like MacKenzie and Stirling, his mother and father and sisters. He thought also of Elizabeth, but the arrogant features of Ruairidh MacKenzie, the rogue she had run off with, kept appearing in his mind when he did so.

*

At the same time, MacKenzie sat in his study in Libberton's Wynd with a glass of whisky in hand and his dog Macrae sitting obediently at his side. His thoughts were of his daughter, as he gazed into the flickering flames of the fire. Her absence was a physical pain that the whisky could only slightly numb. He had received a letter from his brother. There was still no word of her in the north, only rumours of armies marching and the price of grain rising and everyone fearful and uncertain about what they should do. He sighed, picked up the earthenware bottle of whisky on the table and filled his glass again. He raised it and gave a short toast in Gaelic before downing it. He closed his eyes, savouring the familiar burning feeling in his throat and gullet, as the wind beat the shutters and the rain lashed the city. He had no thoughts for the weather outside. He cared nothing for wind or rain, thunder or lightning. It was of no consequence compared to the pain in his heart. Grief washed through him like a wave, grief for the loss of his wife years before and a sharper grief for the loss of his only daughter. And the additional selfish thought behind his grief of a long, lonely old age also arose in his mind.

All of a sudden, it was there before him again, as it had appeared so many times over the years since her death: a black speck in the distance in his mind's eye, becoming a bird against the white sky, flying towards him, growing larger, until the bird was a vortex spinning in his mind and he was aware of a knot in his stomach. It became a sharp pain and nausea flooded through him. The vortex became a pit which opened up around him. The darkness was waiting to take him. He peered down into it. He felt an overwhelming desire to let himself fall. To end his life would be blessed relief. An end to pain. There was a loaded gun in his desk. It was only a few paces across the room. He could turn it on his head and blow his brains out and then there would be nothing. No more pain. But what if Elizabeth returned to find him destroyed? He saw her standing alone at his graveside, alone in the world, an orphan without mother or father. If he died now, he would abandon her. His rational self recoiled from the pit's magnetic pull. His spirit for action returned. He walked away from it. He could not succumb to it. He must fight with every fibre, for her sake. The whisky was now washing through his blood. He felt a little better. The black bird flew back into the distance and perched on a solitary tree.

The deluge lasted all night. It swelled the rivers and streams and burns and waterways from Linton in the west to Dunbar in the east and as far as Fala in the south. It flooded the low-lying ground and forced livestock up onto higher pastures. It destroyed crops and damaged farm buildings, as well as washing away bridges on the Tyne, Esk and Avon – a sudden summer storm that had come from nowhere and had left just as suddenly. It would be remembered by generations to come and noted by those who kept diaries, as if, in some way, the weather was directly connected to the momentous political events of the time. In the morning, all was calm. The wind dropped to nothing, the flags in the gardens of the city barely moved. The clouds fled to the sea, leaving the sky above the drenched city an ecstatic blue. Everything dazzled in the sunshine. The city was full of vast puddles and pools. Children made rafts and sailed the Seven Seas in fields around the city. Edinburgh was a city of shining light. The people emerged from the sodden night into a beautiful summer's day, a glorious warm day of calm sunshine.

Just outside the city, not far from the quarry of Craigleith, Dod Shanks wandered aimlessly through the soaking landscape like Noah after the Flood. What a night it had been! He had feared the roof of his house would be blown away. There were so many leaks in it, every pot and pan he owned was employed on the floor to stop it being soaked. The quarry, his place of work, was flooded and could not be entered safely until the water drained away. He had been sent by the master to gauge the damage around the quarry, in case the storm had opened up any rock faces which might be dug for good sandstone in the future. He walked slowly, enjoying the sun on his face and the absence of physical graft. He thanked God for the leisure, even if it was only a day, it was welcome. Beside a small wood on a higher piece of land about half a mile from the quarry, he noticed a pile of rubble. A landslide caused by the deluge had brought down rocks and boulders, leaving a clean face of rock about twenty feet in height. It was a small cliff which had not been there the day before. Roots of trees could be seen from underneath. He was reminded of the frightening power of nature. What was God trying to tell them? He was surely displeased with the nation turning against its rightful King and installing a Dutch impostor. He closed his eyes for a moment and prayed Dundee would have success in the Highlands and cast the Presbyterians asunder.

As he approached the cliff, he noticed something lying at the bottom. From a distance, it looked like a large, black sack among the debris. But as he got closer he realised it was a human body, dark and heavy from the soaking, lying face down in the mud. His first thought was to run back to tell the master. Then another thought passed through his mind. He knew it was a selfish, sleekit one, but he could not help it. His wife was pregnant again. These were hard times. Money was short. What if there was something valuable on the body? His master would take it for himself – why should his master benefit from the man's misfortune and not him?

He got down beside the body and began to search the pockets of the breeches and jacket. A stink of decay rose from the corpse. The man was not freshly dead. He looked down at the remains of a young face and noticed that the man had worn a wig. As he moved the head slightly to one side, he saw a dark gash across the throat from one side to the other and recoiled. A knife had slashed the man's life away, he had not fallen in the flood or died of natural causes, he had been slain. The thought hastened his search of the pockets. He grabbed something from an inside pocket of the jacket. It was a lump of paper congealed in mud, and stuffed it into his own. He was disappointed not to find any metal, any coin. He moved quickly away in case anyone was watching. He found himself on his feet again, marching back to the quarry. He would examine what he had found later, but he had low expectations. There was no gold or silver as he had hoped. There was nothing heavy weighing down his pocket like a guinea or piece of eight.

CHAPTER 3

The Office of Mrs Hair

SHE LOOKED UP FROM behind the large tome resting on her desk. She was a tiny woman dressed plainly in a black frock. A prim little face lined with age, a head encased in a white bonnet. 'Still no word of him, Mr Galbraith?' she asked pleasantly.

Galbraith stood at the other side of the desk. He was a tall, thin man who stooped slightly, dressed in black breeches and jacket. 'None, madam,' he replied lugubriously, depositing a pile of documents.

'How long has he been gone now?' she asked.

'Five days, madam. There's no sign of him anywhere. I've called at his chambers twice myself. His landlord says he's not seen him for a week. The boy's been all over town looking for him – his usual haunts, favourite taverns and coffee houses. He's disappeared into thin air!'

'Very unlike Mr MacLeod. He was always early in the office, always busy, although he was canny. I sense he had some business of his own on the go, Mr Galbraith. What do you think?'

'I don't know about that, madam. I wasn't privy to his personal dealings. I agree it's unlike him to be… to be so silent. He is always talking about something, always laughing at something or someone.'

'Maybe his own business has taken him away for a few days. But why not tell anyone? Is he off to the Highlands, perhaps? Highlanders can be a law unto themselves. They do things differently there. He may pop up in a day or two with a few cows in tow from the Falkirk fair. You know, Mr Galbraith, a Highland client once paid me with a beast, escorted all the way from the Highlands and presented in the High Street outside my office,' she said, smiling.

Galbraith smiled back, nervously. He could never quite relax in her company, despite having served her for years. She was pleasant enough to him. She was a good mistress, although sharp when roused. MacLeod was a sly one, though. He did not want to say it to her. Hard working – yes, he was that all right – but furtive, always up to something. He had a score of other ventures on the go, he was sure of that – he had seen him in strange company more than once. And there were rumours he was a Jacobite, and an active one at that, not just one of those who toasted the old King's health after a pint of wine in the tavern. He was a plotting and planning Jacobite, and that made him dangerous to know. But he said nothing of this to Mrs Hair. He just nodded in agreement. There was nothing wrong with it, anyway. King James was the rightful King of Scotland. William had seized the throne illegally by force, invading the country with a huge army like William the Conqueror. He himself had no desire to fight to bring the old King back. James was a Papist after all and Edinburgh folk had little use for the Whore of Babylon.

'Keep me informed of everything, Mr Galbraith,' she barked in a sharper tone, then softened as she removed her spectacles to reveal tiny, piercing blue eyes. 'Now tell me, how's your wife?'

'She's as well as can be expected, madam. She's due in a few weeks. Our second bairn.'

'I wish her god speed and a safe delivery. It's a worrying time for you all. I pray God looks after you.' She turned to gaze out the small sash window which looked down on the High Street. She was lost in her own thoughts for a few moments.

Before Galbraith had a chance to answer, before he had the chance to say he was sorry for her losses, as he had done many times before, she dropped her eyes to her papers, and replaced her tiny, round spectacles, which told him she was done with small talk. 'Back to business, Mr Galbraith. We have money to make. Time is money.'

He was relieved to be discharged with a flick of a gloved hand. She was a force to be reckoned with all right, old Mrs Hair, or Mary Erskine, as she was still called by the older merchants. Erskine was her maiden name, but most called her Mrs Hair, the name of her second husband. If she ran a tight ship, she was always fair, at least that was the way she'd been with him over the years he'd served her. She was the sharpest blade he'd come across in the field of business. She never missed a trick. She had an eye for every bawbee in a transaction, every word in a letter or instrument. She would pick up the slightest mistake. He had seen many clerks humiliated by her eye for detail. The transposition of an 's' or 'p', a full stop missed out, a name misspelt. But she did not pick on then afterwards, as many would have done. She said the only way to learn in life was to make mistakes and remember them. That is what she had done. She had made many mistakes, she always said.

CHAPTER 4

An Incident in the Canongate

SCOUGALL TOOK A SIP of wine, then tucked into the venison pie on his plate. He had a ferocious appetite. He was more and more like his old self. He was sleeping better each night; the nightmares less frequent. He looked down at a belly protruding over his belt. He was putting on weight. 'A guid belly on you for the winter, that's what you need, Davie Scougall,' his mother told him, seriously. She was glad to see him growing fat again. With his rising appetite, the lassitude which had afflicted him during the winter and spring was diminishing. He thought less and less of Agnes. He had fallen for her, then she had betrayed him, disappearing off to America with her brother. To his surprise, the journey to the Highlands with MacKenzie had helped his recovery, although it was full of things he disliked: sailing, he was violently sea-sick on the ship from Leith to the Black Isle, the first long sea-journey of his life, which met rough seas off Aberdeen; hunting, a deer hunt with the MacKenzie clan in the hills, when he spent a whole day on horseback, wrapped in a filthy plaid, an exhausting experience as he was not skilled on a horse; and whisky – he did not have a taste for the pungent drink but pretended to savour it to please his host, MacKenzie's elder brother Simon. He had been violently sick the next morning. The overall effect of the trip, however, which he had not enjoyed at the time, he saw now, was a positive one. It had forced himself out of himself, shifted his mind away from painful memories of the deceitful Agnes Morrison and his incarceration in the Harlequin's lair when he had looked death in the face. He was looking to the future again. He had enjoyed meeting MacKenzie's brother and his family at Ardcoul Castle.

He was soon to meet a Musselburgh lass arranged by his mother and his desire for golf was returning. He was also on sound terms with MacKenzie following their political disagreements of the previous year. Scougall supported the Revolution which had brought William and Mary to the throne and sent James into exile. MacKenzie did not. He had learned from his experiences during the Revolution that involvement in politics brought nothing but trouble. He would keep well away from the dirty business in future. But he could not help reflecting positively on recent developments and hoped MacKay would deal quickly with the rebel Dundee. Then all would be well, although he must remember not to scoff in front of MacKenzie when the Jacobites were finally crushed in battle. He would keep off the subject of politics. He knew MacKenzie had no liking for King William – he was no doubt a Jacobite at heart, if not in action. MacKenzie was fighting a more painful battle. The trail had run cold for his daughter Elizabeth in the chaos enveloping the Highlands. Scougall wondered if she was already wed to Ruairidh MacKenzie. He prayed it had not happened, but feared her soul already belonged to the Antichrist.

Stirling returned to the table having relieved himself outside in the close. Scougall noticed his unhealthy pallor. While he, himself, had gained weight, Stirling was wasting away. He was not his usual self. It was maybe his sudden change of circumstances. Many had been disturbed by the political changes of the last year – the whole fabric of the nation shaken. Stirling appeared disgruntled and unsettled by it all. Perhaps the greatest change in him was how little he now spoke of the subject he usually bored every listener about – his writing of his History of the Great Rebellion and his hero Montrose. It was as if he had faded since his fall from office, becoming a ghost of his previous self. Perhaps, as MacKenzie feared, he was ill. How the world was changed since William landed at Torbay the previous November. Even the mighty Lord Advocate Rosehaugh had been swept from office, replaced by Dalrymple, Master of Stair. Many Scottish nobles, disgusted by the events, had joined the deposed King overseas. It was rumoured James was now in Ireland. Edinburgh was in a state of turmoil: armed men marching relentlessly up and down the streets and an insatiable hunger for news, with screams of excitement every time a messenger arrived in the city. Scougall wanted things back to the way they had been before. He yearned for stability and peace, so he could earn money, play golf and find a pretty wife. Instead, there was fear of plots and rebellions, talk of a seizure of the city by Jacobites, or a landing of French soldiers at the Firth. The city was bursting at the seams with Presbyterians who had arrived at the time of the Revolution and had not yet gone home. If the Jacobites were victorious in the Highlands, it would be a disaster. The clans would fall on Edinburgh like wolves and seek revenge by slaying thousands. But MacKay of Scourie was an old war dog. He would surely emerge victorious. God was on their side, after all!

As MacKenzie refilled Scougall's glass with claret, there was a deafening bang from outside. It was so loud the fabric of the Periwig Tavern shook, stopping every customer in their tracks. Scougall thought it sounded like a canon had been fired somewhere in the city. The folk in the tavern looked around at each other nervously. Were they under attack from the Papists? MacKenzie had spilled his wine on the table and was now cursing in Gaelic.

'My God! What was that?' asked Stirling 'Are we under attack from Dundee already? Or is the government firing at something outside the walls?' He looked strangely revived by the explosion. The tavern was in a state of confusion, bordering on panic. Everyone tried to clamber out into the vennel, leaving their food and drink, desperate to find out what had happened.

'Come, gentlemen. I suggest we take the air,' said MacKenzie, taking his hat.

In the narrow vennel, a crowd was swarming up the slope towards the High Street. There were shouts of confusion around them: 'We're under attack from Papist swine', 'Take cover!', 'Jacobites are taking the city!'

Suddenly, everyone stopped in their tracks. Word spread that another cannon had been fired. They backed into the tenement wall. But nothing happened. There was no other explosion. After a couple minutes, the exodus continued, the crowd screaming hatred for the supposed attackers. Above them, from the higher storeys of the tenements, hundreds of heads were sticking out of the windows, desperate to find out if the city was under attack.

They could see no sign of damage in the Lawnmarket, the part of the High Street nearest the castle. People were drifting down towards the Canongate. They followed, swept up in the throng, accompanied by shouts of 'Jacobite Plot! Powder Plot! Explosion in the Canongate! A Powder Plot against King William! A Powder Plot against all good Protestants! Crush the Papist Dogs!'

Scougall took hold of MacKenzie's cuff, stopping him in his tracks. He had just thought of something. 'It might be safer for you to go home to your chambers or back to the Hawthorns, sir,' he said worriedly. 'Until things are calmer. Those suspected of sympathy for the old King might not be treated kindly.' Scougall recalled the violence on the night of the Great Riot the previous December when Edinburgh suffered an orgy of destruction. He had witnessed himself acts of cold-blooded murder and brutal retribution on the High Street. Man was made bestial at such times.

'I want to know what's happened, Davie. This is my city as much as any hot-headed Covenanter from Dumfries!'

Stirling decided to head home. 'Good night, gentlemen. I think I'll heed Davie's warning.'

It was only a five-minute walk down to the Canongate. By the time MacKenzie and Scougall got there, a crowd of a few hundred – fear on many faces, excitement on others – was gathered near Moray House. One side of the High Street was destroyed. An entire tenement block had been brought down. It was fortunately not as high as those near the castle, but three storeys of masonry lay in a vast, smoking pile. It was like a scene from Hell. Relatives of the missing wandered with torches through the rubble. Smashed pieces of furniture lay everywhere in the ruins. Body parts were splattered across the street. It was like a battlefield after an artillery assault. Awful cries of grief were everywhere.

MacKenzie felt despair. It was just as he had feared. Political revolution brought bloody revenge, like a blood feud, slaughter after slaughter, until the nation was saturated in blood, an endless cycle of killings. This was the Whigs' glorious revolution! The reign of King James was over. Now the reign of blood would begin. Fanatics on both sides would carry out atrocities. He cursed the stupidity of James for bringing Scotland to this. He had inherited a realm at peace only a few years before. A little wise policy could have avoided such mayhem. But there was not a drop of wisdom in the cup of that useless Stuart monarch.

CHAPTER 5

The Royal Coffee House

THERE WAS A PAINED expression on Scougall's face the next morning as he sat drinking coffee with MacKenzie and Stirling. He was reading a piece in the *Gazette*.

Edinburgh Gazette *10 July 1689*

'An Awful Explosion in the Canongate'

Robertson's Land in the Canongate was utterly destroyed last night by an awful explosion of gunpowder at ten of the night. The noise of the terrible explosion was heard as far away as the towns of Colinton, Currie and Liberton. The tenement destroyed belonged to merchant Abraham Slight. In the blast, many inhabitants of the city were slain, including Slight himself, his wife Jessie, and servants Alexander Silverman and Ann Taylor. Also among the dead were merchant Andrew Dunlop, Helen Dunlop his daughter, Robbie Dundas writer and Donald MacDonald, Town Guard.

It is suspected that barrels of gunpowder stored in the cellar underneath the tenement caused the explosion. Some say the powder was bought by Slight to supply MacKay's army in the north. Others on the street who the Gazette has spoken with believe it is the work of Jacobites, who discovering where the powder was stored, ignited it like Guy Fawkes and his conspirators, to engender mischief within the city by attacking the government of William and Mary, proclaimed King and Queen a few months ago.

Several others in the tenement and a few passers-by on the High Street were injured in the blast, some are still in danger of their lives.

Lord Advocate Dalrymple has asked that any intelligence about the incident be passed to his office immediately. He told the Gazette all his efforts would be applied to finding out who was behind the dreadful event and bringing those responsible to justice.

Scougall put the paper down on the table. MacKenzie picked it up and began to read.

'Robert Dundas is known to me, sir. Not a close acquaintance, not a friend, but a contemporary. I've known him since we began our apprenticeships. Such a dreadful end to a promising career.'

'Awful, indeed, Davie.' MacKenzie's eyes quickly scanned the story. 'Why do you think he was in the house at the time?'

'I believe he worked for Dunlop. He was probably overseeing some business. He was a well-regarded writer.'

'Dunlop and Slight were rich merchants. This will rock the foundations of the community.' MacKenzie carefully re-read the piece, sipping from his coffee cup now and again. 'Was it a terrible accident or a plot to destabilise the city?' He was impressed by the speed the publication offered the details to the public, despite the confusion of the last twelve hours. A rational intelligence was observing events, recording them, packaging them and selling them. He smiled at Stirling as he handed the paper to him, tapping him on the thigh. 'Our services will not be required this time, Archibald – the Advocate will have little use of suspected Jacobites like us. Do you know anything about Jabb who publishes the *Gazette*, Davie? I hear he's one of your Presbyterians.'

'He's a newcomer to the city,' replied Scougall, slightly annoyed by MacKenzie's jibe at his religious position. 'Not a

Presbyterian, but a non-conformist from London. The *Gazette* sells well. Everyone is hungry for news, especially about Dundee's fortunes in the North. I've heard the first print run sold out in two minutes this morning. But it cannot be right to make money from the misfortune of others.'

'Now he has a real story for his readers. Any news from the North, Archibald?'

Stirling scanned the small print below the piece about the explosion. 'Let me see, John. A body has been found at Craigleith Quarry after the storm. Cause of death unknown. News from the North: nothing new. The armies follow each other in a merry dance. MacKay was camped near Inverness to rest his troops, before following Dundee into the mountains. His aim is to crush his army of savages. Do we face civil war again?'

MacKenzie's face darkened. 'This is civil war and it has spread to Edinburgh already. We thought it was over when the Duke of Gordon surrendered the castle. I pray it will not be as long and bloody as the last one, which I remember only too well. I was a bairn of three when it began and a man of twenty-five at the Restoration. A generation of devastation. A dark time, especially in the Highlands. So much blood shed. Women and children slain, old clan rivalries ignited and inflamed, killings justified by religious conviction, troops slaying with no regard for human life. And here we are again. Armies marching back and forth like the days of Montrose.' MacKenzie was struck again by a question that kept haunting him – was the restoration of the legitimate King, the Stuart King James, worth so much bloodshed? Was it not better to be rid of the House of Stuart for good? They had failed to bring peace and security to Scotland. Father and son had taken their people to the precipice of Hell and pushed them into it. But he thought of the religious enthusiasts who supported William, the beneficiaries of the Revolution. Scotland was caught between the devil and the deep blue sea, neither option appealing. James was a useless king and a Papist one at that. How would he ever be welcomed back by his people if he continued to follow a religion followed by a tiny minority which was anathema to the majority? There was little chance his son would be brought up a Protestant as an exile in the French court.

A feeling of despair washed through him. Scotland was bitterly divided again, which did not bode well for the future, especially relations with England. England would benefit from the division. The country would be manipulated by duplicitous politicians, English and Scots. Many were calling for a closer union, especially the Presbyterians, as a way of locking the two Protestant realms together. Scotland would become a conquered province! The fate of Elizabeth was caught up in the morass. She was perhaps already wed to the arrogant Ruairidh MacKenzie. Anger replaced despair. He thought of thrusting a dirk into Ruairidh's abdomen. But violence only bred violence. How quickly could man become a blood-thirsty beast! He must not let his rational self be conquered by desire for revenge. Hatred would solve nothing. It would also cloud his judgement when he needed lucidity more than anything.

CHAPTER 6

The Road to Tyneford

STIRLING RODE SLOWLY up the road that climbed steeply a couple of miles south of Dalkeith, his mind full of the provisions of the marriage settlement he hoped to secure for his daughter. It would be completed, he hoped, in a matter of days, if all went according to plan. God knew there had been so many delays along the way. It had sapped his energy over the last few months. He was exhausted by it all. His sleep was disturbed every night. He lay awake for hours, his mind abuzz with calculations – how could he afford it all? He was in a continual state of agitation, but Margaret was determined the marriage should go ahead, at any cost. She kept driving him on to the final goal. She would not let it rest day or night, at the table or in the bed chamber – once they had Arabella settled on Dewarton's son, they might relax, she told him, only then might he enjoy his retirement, return to his History, which he had neglected entirely since all this business began. Before all this, he had expected Arabella would marry a neighbouring laird or a rich advocate recommended by MacKenzie or, at worst, a doctor. But this sensible path did not appeal to Arabella or her mother. They must aim far higher. He recalled the conversation at the dinner table only a few months ago, just after his fall from office. It had quite spoiled his dinner. Margaret had heard from some acquaintance that Dewarton's youngest son looked favourably on Arabella, having seen her at a party in Edinburgh, indeed the young fool was infatuated with her. There was a chance, Margaret argued excitedly, with bulging eyes, if they acted swiftly, they might snare an earl's son for their daughter. Arabella might call an earl, father-in-law.

She would live amongst the highest echelons of society as a member of the nobility! Stirling was not pleased when he heard this. His mind immediately turned to money. What would such a match cost? How could they afford the tocher for such a marriage? They no longer had his salary as Crown Officer, nor the perquisites of office, payments obtained now and again, which some might call bribes, but an important lubricant of justice. He had grown used to such fortunate bonuses. His landed estate was not large, and the other funds he possessed, most of which were lent out to nobles, would have to be called back in to cover the marriage portion. He would also have to borrow more. That was a difficult and delicate matter, especially when it was done all at once. It was not sound policy, he told Margaret. They were taking on an almighty risk. They should aim for a more reasonable match, reflecting their financial circumstances and position in society, and, though he did not say this to her, one which would be a lot less bother for him and allow him to get on with enjoying himself, rather than managing tortuous financial transactions which might threaten their long-term wellbeing. Margaret was appalled by his lack of enthusiasm, calling him everything under the sun: a laggard rascal afflicted by lassitude, a preposterous poop dedicated to dry antiquarian pursuits and other terms equally offensive to his sensitive ear. They argued bitterly. She did not speak to him for two days and finally got a tearful Arabella to tell him how much she was set on the match. It was a matter of the heart, rather than just a political match for the family. Dewarton's son was a gentle soul who would make a loyal husband and other such rubbish. They wore him down. They did not let the matter rest, day or night, until, as he was wont, he gave in to them as he had done on countless occasions before, whether about a shopping trip to London or the purchase of a puppy – anything for a quiet life. If they were driven to bankruptcy, it would not be his fault; it would be theirs, although he knew he would still be blamed.

So, he had begun negotiations with a heavy heart, feeling sure it would not end well. Ambitious plans usually came unstuck. And sure enough, the price demanded by the earl's lawyers for the tocher began to rise, despite being on good terms with Dewarton and sharing his political viewpoint. The price was far too high for a younger son of the family. But, the argument went, if the elder brothers died – one was apparently in poor health and the other a soldier who might be slain on the battlefield – the boy would become earl himself and Arabella would be the wife of an earl. Was that not worth paying a substantial price for, Margaret argued, her excitement palpable at the thought of how they would benefit from deaths in the earl's family. What honour and prestige would accrue to the family of Stirling! He had to admit he was affected by such a prospect. His grandchildren would be nobles. The vanity in his character loved the thought of it, but the dominant part of his nature, which tended towards inertia, and had led him countless times to do nothing in the public as well as the private sphere of life, made him cautious and wish they would have nothing to do with it, although he recognised his wife and daughter made this impossible. They were set on the marriage as surely as the sun rose each morning. The negotiations, as he had expected, proved long and hard and at each stage another obstacle kept appearing. He had to work out where he would raise more money from. He decided to conduct everything himself without seeking another lawyer's help. Was he not an advocate after all! Was he not the retired Crown Officer of Scotland! He knew the law of the land! But he was soon driven to distraction by all the documents which had to be written and eventually was forced to employ a writer. He thought of using Scougall, the most exact writer he knew, who was not expensive. But he decided against it. There was something that held him back from using a friend for such a delicate matter. Scougall was a friend, although beneath him in society. Instead, he employed Robbie Dundas, a writer of some skill, who came highly recommended. But disaster had struck! Dundas was killed in the explosion on the High Street. He could not believe his bad fortune. At least most of the legal work was completed. He could finish the remaining deeds himself. Yes, he was giving away far too much. He had been forced to issue bond after bond to raise money to cover the payments. Most of the nobles he had lent money to could not pay him back at such short notice because of the political situation. Most financial transactions were frozen like ice. MacKenzie had raised his eyebrows when he sought to borrow £1,000 from him, but had signed the bond as a true friend, not asking what the money was for. There was no way out of it now. Arabella's expectations were sky high. She claimed she was in love, so how could he crush her hopes by saying they could not afford the match. How could he deny his only daughter? How could cold money come between the lovers! He would have to pay exorbitant interest rates. Dewarton was a slippery eel, but his son appeared reasonable, a promising young man who might prove a loyal and devoted husband, although he doubted it. If he followed in his father's footsteps he would soon be gambling, drinking and whoring, and attending clandestine gatherings to plot the return of the old King.

He reached the top of the long slope and turned his horse to take in the view: the Pentland Hills in the distance beyond Penicuik and the city of Edinburgh to the north, with spires and tenements, the hulk of Arthur's Seat and the grey Firth beyond. His mind drifted to Montrose, his hero since boyhood, as it did less and less during these busy days. Montrose was a man of action. He would not have spent precious time negotiating a marriage. For him, it would have been a trifle, a thing done in an afternoon. He wished he was more like him. At times, he thought he was like him. But he knew his true nature was nothing like him. Montrose would have handed the whole thing over to a lawyer. A man fighting for his life, for his King, for an ideal, needed to focus on other more noble matters. Now another Stuart King was in exile, another war had to be fought to place him back on the throne. Thoughts of Montrose led his mind onto Dundee. Some were already saying Dundee was the new Montrose, at least that is what the Jacobites hoped. A new Montrose would smash the dour MacKay. If he was a younger man, he would have fought alongside him in the Highlands.

Yes, he told himself, on that point there was no doubt in his soul. If he was a younger man, he would have escaped from this confounded marriage business. And if he was called to act for his true King today he would do so. The thought made him feel better about himself and his spirits rose. He had been down in the dumps for weeks. There was at least something in which he could believe. But what was he to do? Bide his time and wait to see what happened in the Highlands? He was already in contact with supporters in the Lothians. History might intervene to change things, completely.

He turned his horse and made for home, following the long straight road southwards, an artery built by the Romans long ago, it was said, down which soldiers marched in their attempt to crush the land in the north. The thought that Romans had reached far off Scotland pleased him, that the Latin tongue was spoken here. His house and family and lands meant everything to him, but there were higher ideals. If it came to it, he would risk everything, just as Montrose had done. He mused further, as his horse plodded on through the rigs. He would risk everything for the cause of the Stuart. He would sacrifice himself just as Montrose had done. He was lost in his fantasies until he found himself looking down on the little village of Tyneford nestling beside the Tyne Water and the house among the tall trees. It was a beautiful spot, a sanctuary from the city, a sanctuary from the world of politics, a sanctuary from the world of money.

CHAPTER 7

A Request from the Clan MacLeod

MACKENZIE WAS WANDERING around the garden at the Hawthorns, his country house to the west of Edinburgh. The herbaceous borders were at their peak, a multitude of blooming flowers. The scent of a rose stopped him in his tracks as he walked down the path. The memory of his pregnant wife standing with him in this very spot, one of his last days with her, although he did not know at the time, suddenly came to mind. He got a flash of the bird perched on the black branch but he forced it out of his mind. He reflected that he had devoted little time to the garden since Elizabeth had run off. With her gone, it was diminished somehow. He plodded down the path and sat on a bench beside the wall in the shade, taking up a copy of the *Gazette* he carried in his hand.

The Edinburgh Gazette *12 July 1689*

'An Awful Explosion Revisited'

Two days ago, the city was rocked by a huge explosion at the tenement of Abraham Slight which brought the whole structure down, causing fear and consternation across the town and beyond.

Since then, many rumours have circulated about the cause of this devastating blow to the fabric of the city. It is feared that it was a heinous attempt by supporters of the late King James, called Jacobites and traitors by the law-loving people of this land, to attack the royal supporters of his beloved Majesties King William and Queen Mary at a critical juncture in the attempt to crush the Rebellion in the Highlands led by John Graham of Claverhouse, wrongly called Viscount Dundee, inveterate traitor.

The Gazette has visited the site of the explosion and talked with many of those in the vicinity who witnessed it and who knew those killed and injured. From this, a number of things have been discerned which we present to our readers:

The explosion was caused by barrels of gunpowder stored in the cellars of the tenement. The powder was brought from Leith the day before by cart and stored in three barrels. It was recently purchased by the government to supply MacKay's troops in their attempt to crush the rebels in the north. In this way, not only have his loyal supporters been killed, but a large amount of good powder used up, which would have helped his Majesty's troops.

The owner of the tenement Abraham Slight was a follower of the Presbyterian creed; a careful and well-regarded merchant of the city for many years and a man loved by all.

Alexander Silverman, the loyal long-standing servant of Slight, also slain.

Robbie Dundas, writer in the city, a young man of much promise and held in high regard by his fellow notaries public and by all those who dealt with him, slain at the tender age of twenty-five.

Andrew Dunlop merchant, another upstanding member of the community, and his wife of forty years Helen Dunlop both killed.

Donald MacDonald, a Town Guard, killed on the street outside the tenement.

Also injured in the explosion was Andrew Stein, Captain of the Town Guard, who walked beside

MacDonald and was lucky not to be killed himself.

It is said Dunlop was heavily in debt to Mrs Mary Hair, formerly known as Mary Erskine. It is believed she will buy the premises. She has said she will rebuild them at her own expense.

The Gazette has learned from a witness that a man was seen coming out of the cellars of the tenement just a few minutes before the explosion. He is described as a tall, dark man with a pock-marked face. It is believed he is responsible for igniting the powder. He was behaving furtively and ran away quickly from the scene.

The news from the North continues to be confused and contradictory. After resting his army for a few days, MacKay follows Dundee through the hills. With God's help, he will crush the rebels. The Gazette will continue to provide readers with more details in the next edition.

MacKenzie shut his eyes, enjoying the warm sunshine on his face. When he opened them, his servant Meg was approaching down the path, carrying something in her hand – perhaps a letter. His heart started pounding. Could it be from Elizabeth? He took it expectantly and ripped it open. His heart sank. It was not her hand. It was a message from David Drummond, a lawyer in Edinburgh. Drummond wanted to meet him in the Targe Tavern at two o'clock in the afternoon the next day. Drummond was known as a supporter of the old King who was deeply engaged in plotting his return to the throne. He acted as the man of business of the Drummond brothers, Melfort and Perth, both despised former ministers in the government of King James. Spies would no doubt be on Drummond's tail. Why did Drummond want to see him? Was he being sounded out as a possible supporter of the old King's cause? His heart sank further. He had enough on his plate with Elizabeth. But

Drummond was an old colleague in the Faculty of Advocates. They had served in the Session for twenty years together. They were not friends but acquaintances of a kind, although he had not seen much of him recently. Drummond was also a Gaelic speaker. It would be dishonourable not to accept the invitation of a fellow Highlander and, besides, he might have information about the armies in the Highlands and know something of Ruairidh MacKenzie's movements. He could not afford to leave any stone unturned as far as Elizabeth was concerned. He scribbled a short reply agreeing to meet him, picking Drew Cameron's rather than the Targe, a less popular howff.

Returning to Edinburgh the next day, MacKenzie found Drummond in a dark corner at the back of the tavern. Drummond, a well-dressed man with a freshly powdered wig and of similar age to MacKenzie, ordered a bottle of seck, and looked around furtively before speaking softly in Gaelic. 'Thank you for seeing me, John. It's been too long since we shared a bottle. These are difficult days, indeed. I believe we have not spoken since his Majesty departed last November. These are dark days for the House of Stuart. I am so busy with… business…' Drummond looked around again suspiciously before continuing. 'I'll get straight to the point. You'll have heard of the discovery of a body near Craigleith Quarry a few days ago?'

'I think there was a brief description in the *Gazette*,' replied MacKenzie after sipping his wine.

'The body has been identified as Aeneas MacLeod, a young writer in Mrs Hair's office. As you may know, I advise his father, Roderick MacLeod of Rhenigidale. It's a terrible shock for him and the clan MacLeod, indeed for all God-fearing men who are friends of the MacLeods. The body lay buried under the ground for days before it was found. I had the dreadful task of identifying him myself. His end was brutal; his throat cut from ear to ear. The body was dumped in a pit near the quarry where it would have remained in perpetuity had not a landslide caused by the storm disturbed the earth. He was found by a quarryman the morning after. God surely acts in mysterious ways. He may have lain undisturbed for a thousand years! The body is in the morgue waiting for his family to take him back to the Highlands to be laid to rest.'

MacKenzie nodded and refilled their glasses. 'Why have you asked to meet me, David?'

'I'll get straight to the point, John. The case is hardly considered by the Advocate. Dalrymple shows no interest in it. He hums and haws but does absolutely nothing. The clan believe it is because Aeneas was not a Presbyterian. Perhaps understandably at a time of civil strife, the government has other things to concern itself with. But it's a great dishonour to the MacLeods that no one should investigate the killing properly.'

MacKenzie listened attentively, pleased to have something else to focus his attention on rather than his missing daughter. He always found peculiar appeal in the facts of a murder – unlike much else in life, there was a certain kind of clarity to be gained from investigating an unnatural death. It was often a story devoid of complexity. A man was killed by another man or women. That was a pure fact. How was the person killed? What weapon was used? Where and when did the killing occur? Why did it happen? The body was moved to the place of burial. How was that done? These were all facts which could be worked out from evidence. As his mind buzzed with questions, he could feel his melancholy fade. Whether the victim was Jacobite or Williamite, was just a fact to be added to the rest, a detail which could account for the death, but which he did not have to take a position on himself. In a strange way, there was moral purity about a murder. He took another sip of wine. 'Why have you told me all this?' he asked.

Drummond looked around nervously again before continuing in Gaelic. 'My client seeks your services, John. You are known to be good at such things. Since your fall from office, you will not be as busy as you were. The courts are closed. Lawyers have time on their hands. Many return to their estates and await political developments.'

'I still have plenty of work to be getting on with,' replied MacKenzie. 'I've clients across the land, especially in the Highlands. You can imagine there's much business to do for them at the moment. The work is not as lucrative as the Session, but there's always something, a debt to be arranged, a wadset negotiated, a marriage settlement brokered, the education of a son organised.' He smiled to himself. It was all dull, plodding work. He missed the drama of the Session, the comradeship of other lawyers, the gossip, the feeling of being at the centre of things.

'Such things are trifles, John! I know you've helped Stirling in other cases. We need your help. MacLeod of Rhenigidale requests your help. The great MacLeod of Dunvegan demands your help!' Drummond's face broke into a smile at this point. 'Dalrymple cares little for the case. He's focused entirely on political matters. His sole aim is to destroy support for King James in the city. He has no interest in the process of law until political matters are settled, particularly the unnatural death of a man believed to be a Jacobite and so an inveterate enemy of the government. From Dalrymple's point of view, one less traitor roams the streets. He has one less traitor to spy on. The MacLeods want someone to investigate the killing. They want justice for Aeneas. The kin of Aeneas MacLeod demand it. They are incensed that no one cares about his death. It's not just the death of an Edinburgh lawyer, it's the killing of the heir to the estate of Rhenigidale in Harris, the killing of a member of the MacLeod gentry, and the kindred which owes allegiance to MacLeod of Dunvegan. The great MacLeod himself is devastated. Aeneas was fostered with him as a boy. He was very fond of his dear foster child.' Drummond sipped his wine before continuing: 'You'll be paid for your services. It will also, naturally, cement the close ties of kinship which already bind the clans of MacKenzie and MacLeod.'

MacKenzie nodded, seriously. He was delighted by the offer, but could not say so immediately. Etiquette required he take his time. After sipping his wine and pondering for a few moments, his expression lightened: 'It's an honour to be asked by MacLeod of Dunvegan.' He tried not to seem too keen, but he was excited at the prospect of an investigation. A case would distract his attention from his daughter. It would also give him an excuse to disengage from politics and focus all his attention elsewhere. He raised his glass. 'Tell MacLeod I'll take the case. I'll do all I can to identity the killer of Aeneas MacLeod. Now, tell me everything you know about him.'

Drummond talked on in Gaelic, providing the following details over another bottle of wine which MacKenzie later described to Scougall over a further bottle in the Periwig that evening. 'We have a case to be getting on with, Davie. Something to distract us.'

Scougall put his glass down and turned his full attention to MacKenzie. He was also pleased to have something else to think about.

'The description in the *Gazette* was curt. A body was found at Craigleith Quarry. Cause of death unknown. We now know it was the body of Aeneas MacLeod, son of Roderick MacLeod of Rhenigidale in Harris. He was apprenticed as a writer in Edinburgh to George Hutchison at the age of fourteen. I believe he was a few years older than you. He was groomed to be clan lawyer of the MacLeods of Dunvegan. In time he would look after all the legal and financial affairs of the clan. Aeneas spent seven years in the household of MacLeod as a child and was loved by the chief. The custom of fosterage is still followed in some clans, although less common as the world changes. You may recall I was fostered myself as a boy. My memories of that time are among the happiest of my life. A deep bond is forged between foster child and foster parents. MacLeod loved Aeneas as his own child, he is devastated by his death. He seeks justice for him.'

'I knew Aeneas slightly, sir. He was a skilled writer,' said Scougall, recalling also that he thought that MacLeod was an arrogant upstart who looked down on everyone.

'After completing his apprenticeship with Hutchison he took a position, surprisingly, in the office of Mrs Hair. There he acted as a book keeper, gaining knowledge of the specialties of her office: bond trading and property transactions, as well as funding domestic and foreign trade. According to Drummond, he also looked after a small book of his own loans. In other words, he was building up his own business. From his work for Mrs Hair, he would establish useful contacts, while acting at the same time as the MacLeod clan lawyer. At some point, he would've left her office and made his own way. There was something else Drummond did not mention to me directly. I know from my contacts that Aeneas was an active Jacobite, involved in raising funds for the old King. It's a position supported by MacLeod of Dunvegan and many other chiefs troubled by the Revolution and, particularly, the return of the Earl of Argyll in the Prince of Orange's train. You will know well, Davie, that Argyll is hated by many clans.'

Scougall was trying to recall the times he had met MacLeod over the years. It was a shock that another contemporary of his was dead, first Robbie Dundas and now MacLeod. He had come across MacLeod a few times over the years. He had done business with most notaries in Edinburgh as they were a relatively small community. 'I must admit, sir, I didn't care for him.' Scougall did not like speaking ill of the dead but knew he had to speak plainly to MacKenzie if they were investigating a death.

MacKenzie raised his eyebrows. 'Why not, Davie? It is unlike you to be so blunt.'

'I thought he was arrogant on the few occasions that my work brought us together.' Scougall found it difficult to divulge how he really felt about him. He stuttered on. 'I felt MacLeod looked down on me as an ignorant Lowlander with... with the arrogance common in some Highlanders who consider themselves nobles even though they don't belong to the titled aristocracy.' Scougall feared he had gone too far in his criticism of Highlanders but MacKenzie just nodded, thoughtfully.

'There are good and bad Highlanders, Davie. We must find out as much as we can about him.'

Scougall noticed that MacKenzie looked in better spirits than he had done since the disappearance of Elizabeth. Colour had returned to his cheeks and there was a sparkle of enthusiasm in his dark eyes.

'We don't have to like him,' MacKenzie continued. 'But it's our job to find out what happened to him. Here's what we know so far. MacLeod's body was found the day after the great storm near Craigleith Quarry by a quarryman. During the night, a landslide brought down a rock face, which spilled out his body. It now lies in the morgue, being held there until his father arrives to take him back to the clan lands for burial. We'll need to examine the body ourselves. According to Drummond, MacLeod's throat was cut and he was buried in an unmarked grave.' MacKenzie stopped to allow Scougall to digest the basic details. He took out his pipe and lit it, engulfing the table in a cloud of smoke. 'Do you have any questions, Davie?'

Scougall tried to contain his disgust for smoking. 'Do you think the killing is connected with MacLeod's political position, to his support of the old King?'

MacKenzie lowered his voice and looked around the tavern surreptitiously. 'It's possible. MacLeod was known to be a supporter of James. But we must wait and see what the evidence tells us. Let us be led by what we find, not our prejudices about MacLeod.' MacKenzie raised his glass and smiled. '*Slàinte mhath!*' Then, after taking a large mouthful of wine, said: 'How busy are you in the coming days?'

Before Scougall had time to answer, MacKenzie had taken his hat from the table and was on his way out, shouting back. 'Meet me outside the Tollbooth at ten o'clock tomorrow morning and don't forget your notebook. Tomorrow, we begin a new case.'

CHAPTER 8

Reflections of Mrs Hair

GALBRAITH BROUGHT DISTURBING news, but it was not unexpected. MacLeod was dead.

'It was not an accident, madam. They say it was murder.'

Mrs Hair dropped her quill, spilt a little ink. She never spilt ink. She dismissed Galbraith. She needed to think, alone. She waited until he had closed the door.

Galbraith was reliable if unimaginative, she thought. In an office, you needed all kinds of folk, dull and passionate, reliable and forgetful, quick and slow, bringing balance so the place might function efficiently. MacLeod was one of the passionate ones, perhaps too passionate. He had been useful to her, if not entirely trustworthy. He was passionate for his own interest. However, he had a good head for business, perhaps the only thing they had had in common, and knew the value of Highland land. And now he was dead.

She turned to look at the sky through the window. Business was the only thing that made her forget. Business vanquished the painful thoughts that haunted her every day. Business pushed the little faces out of her mind, the tiny beautiful faces of her five dead bairns. Five dead bairns. She had given birth to them all. It seemed so long ago, like another world, as if they were born from another woman. Five times she had experienced the agony of childbirth and then watched them fade to nothing. She had prayed with all her heart for God to preserve each one. Each was taken for some reason she could not fathom, only known to God himself. She had asked many times how He could allow such suffering for nothing. How He allowed the deaths of so many innocents. Was it because she had sinned? She admitted to herself, although to no other, she had sinned. She was a sinner, as were all God's creatures. Was that the reason they were taken from her? But it was divine Providence; God's business, not hers. They had all died, but she lived on. She had survived two dead husbands. There would be no more of them. That was as certain as death. She'd had enough of men, lying with them as bedfellow, being told what to do in bed and business. They were taken from her as well. Her grief for them was nothing compared to the burning grief for her bairns. She did not know if she had loved either of her husbands. She had certainly not loved the first, although she had grown fond of the second. The first had been her father's choice. She would never have chosen such a grotesque man. He seemed ancient when she had first seen him, although he was only in his thirties when they married. She had feared disagreeing with her father. She had gone along with it without complaining, although she had privately shed tears with her mother. There were many more tears after she had first seen the repulsive creature and smelt the reek of him that she had never gotten used to. The early days of her first marriage were torture. But, thank God, he was taken from her.

Her second husband was much less disagreeable to look at. He was handsome. She was attracted by his good looks. He was little more than a boy when they married. She led him to her bed, rather than a lamb to the slaughter like the first time. Yes, with her second marriage, she had made sure that she was in charge. At least there was pleasure with the second, a little recompense for all the suffering and humiliation of her first marriage, a little recompense for the years that had tasted like flint.

She had found, unexpectedly, that she had an aptitude for business. After her first bedfellow had left her in so much debt – he was a fool with money – she was forced to learn quickly or sink. Her second husband had been more careful and was led by her advice. They had prospered together; he as a druggist and she as a moneylender.

When her second husband died, she was left with a capital fund of her own, not a fortune, but enough to get by. She was free of debt with capital that she controlled. She established an office in her own name. By that time there was a book of loans. She could live off the interest if she was cautious. She became a merchant lady in her own right, one of the few in the city of Edinburgh, and thrived. She became her own woman for the first time since leaving Garlet House as a girl. She would never again be ruled by men. She would never marry again. She had no more need of men, they only wished to rule her and obtain her wealth. She had had suitors in the years following the death of Mr Hair. She thought of a few of them: Dunlop and Slight and Corse. All were repulsive to her. She knew they were not attracted by her tiny body, it was her money they were after. She felt a burning hatred for all the men who had crossed her over the years. She had risen by careful management. She found she was good at business, much better than the fools who called themselves merchants, or the money men who were supposed to understand the direction of the Exchange, but always bought or sold at the wrong time. And now they were begging her for funds. Now they wanted money and she possessed it, so the price she charged for it rose. She could not deny such power gave her pleasure, the most pleasure she had experienced in a long life of pain. It made life bearable, but it was no real antidote to the small faces crowding her mind, especially in the evenings when she sat alone at the fire. They were like small birds in the nest seeking the food of love. They were her constant travelling companions in the journey of life. Would she meet them again in the afterlife, her little darlings? And what kind of creatures would they be? Stillborn bairns or full-grown souls? The question accompanied her waking hours. She could not make any sense of it. God did not provide assurance for her. What was the nature of the afterlife? Would she still be a woman there? Or would her soul be free of the constraints of sex? Would God allow her this? She prayed with all her heart it would be so. In her dreams, she was with them again, their tiny bodies cuddled against her, seeking her breast across eternity. In her dreams, she played with them in the summer sunshine in the garden at Garlet House and told them stories after tucking them into bed.

Her thoughts returned to MacLeod and business, once more. She knew what the good merchants of Edinburgh really thought of her. They were her inveterate enemies. They had opposed her at every turn through the years. She had learned from an early stage what she needed to survive as a merchant maiden: news was vital. Knowledge was power. She paid for intelligence about her competitors, whilst they knew nothing about it. She had built up a long list of informants over the years. Some were now on their last legs themselves, much older than her. Some still inhabited the drinking dens she never entered. They soaked up news from the city and offered it to her. The process always started with a little chat around town, before a deal was completed. Then they came back to her to provide snippets of news. She would never pay a huge amount for the news, but just enough to make it worth the informants' while, so they came back to her first. She was surprised to learn some men dealt solely in the business of others. There was always dirt clinging to men. There was always clart on a merchant's shoes. She was always surprised by how often those appearing holy in public were driven by perversions. Hypocrisy was like the wind in Edinburgh, waiting around every corner. When she was ready, she would challenge them. She would have revenge upon them and they would never know she was responsible. The thought passed through her mind that she might be killed by one of them. She had feared it more than once in a long career as merchant maiden. She had almost desired it in her days of acutest grief. But she rarely had to use force in her years of money lending; only once or twice in thirty years had she hired a strong arm. The threat was usually enough. If she was slain, it would not be a man who benefitted anyway. Her testament would ensure it. She had formed a plan that she had shared with few, a great plan to establish an educational institution in the city in her name, funded by her legacy. It would ensure girls were educated as well as boys. The place would help daughters of the city, a legacy worth fighting for, allowing them to rise like she had done, but with a helping hand as she never had; a sisterhood of educated women who might free themselves from the grasping hands of men. She would have done some good for the weaker vessel in the eyes of God, and her reward might be to join her lost bairns in the next life. She hoped for this with all her heart.

Thinking of MacLeod again, she mused that he had been useful to her. His death was not unexpected – she had thought, when they had first met, that he would either rise high or fall early. She had spotted his usefulness from the outset. She had overheard him in conversation on the High Street. He was already a canny operator despite his youth. He had political connections and a sharp mind. She was sure he was a Jacobite. She knew the names of other conspirators in the city. She knew the times and places they met. She knew he had other unsavoury contacts. He courted the dregs of the town. They too could prove useful. She wondered if he had pushed one of them too far, one of the figures who operated in the shadows, in the underworld beyond commerce, law and church. If only he had kept his hands away from Betty.

CHAPTER 9

A Conversation with Archibald Stirling

MACKENZIE PUT DOWN the news sheet and called for more drinks. He was sitting at his usual table in the Periwig Tavern with Scougall and Stirling. It was mid-morning and there were only a few customers inside. 'What do you make of the *Gazette* as a publication, Archibald?'

Stirling eyed the news sheet suspiciously. 'I care little for it, John, although I hear it sells well. Everyone is hungry for the news it supplies, although, I must say, a somewhat one-sided account, particularly of events in the Highlands. It's abundantly clear the author does not favour the true King. Some say Jabb is a creature of William, sent north to help his cause, a spy in the pay of the government, with all expenses paid. I believe those who support the old King must counter his assertions but it's difficult when the government licences all publications.'

MacKenzie nodded, then asked: 'Donald MacDonald was killed in the explosion and Captain Stein injured. I presume you know them both?'

Stirling looked distracted for a moment. He drank some ale and belched, before dabbing his lips with his neck cloth. 'Captain Andrew Stein goes by the name of Stein, just Stein. He was a soldier by trade, a tough man, with long experience of war and capable, very capable. MacDonald was a useless imbecile good for two things only – drinking a hogshead of wine and pissing it down a vennel! He was feeble in a fight and could not shoot straight, even with his own member!'

'There are many such men in the Highlands and Lowlands, Archibald,' chuckled MacKenzie. He reflected that Stirling was in a particularly morose mood. Seated on the other side of

MacKenzie, Scougall watched Stirling's long, pale face. Scougall reflected that Stirling had aged since leaving office. The colour had drained from him; his enthusiasm for everything lacking, his cynicism raised to a new pitch.

'Stein's been with the Guard a couple of years,' Stirling continued. 'He fought in various battles, the names of which I cannot recall; some say with Claverhouse himself. He's one of the few in the Guard who can handle a sword and musket. Most are worthless creatures like MacDonald, barely able to speak a word of Scots. Stein is a different kettle of fish. He has experience of the killing business from his time as a soldier. I was surprised he sought the position of Captain. I'm sure he could've taken more lucrative work in the retinue of a nobleman or another country's army as a mercenary. He told me he had sickened of soldiering, all the slaughter and mayhem and taking orders from officers who had paid for commissions. He demonstrated how he could swing a sword and hit a target with a musket at fifty yards. I had no hesitation in employing him and promoting him to captain and, although the rest of the crew moaned about his sudden rise, they were soon taking orders without question.' Stirling took up his tankard again and laughed. 'It's one of the few benefits of retirement – I no longer have to supervise that rabble. I was the one blamed for their incompetence. No one ever had a good word to say about them. Not only were they incompetent, they were completely duplicitous. They took bribes from anyone with a bawbee. Stein continues to improve them by training them in the use of weapons and establishing some discipline. It will do the town good, perhaps.'

'Do you think he was a target of the explosion?' asked Scougall.

'I don't think so, Davie,' replied Stirling. 'The *Gazette* says he was passing by and injured by chance. He was probably just unlucky. If there was a target, which is uncertain as it could've been an accident – it was either Dunlop or Slight – rich men with enemies.'

'I'm well acquainted with Slight. I thought he dealt mostly in cloth. The arms trade is surely new for him,' replied MacKenzie.

'Many merchants hope to benefit from our present difficulties. If the war in the north lasts, or spreads to the Lowlands, the demand for powder will explode. Excuse the pun. The price will rise precipitously. Merchants here buy powder and arms in Amsterdam to sell to the government. Some hold onto their stock, expecting the price to rise further. The profits of the trade are significant.' Stirling sighed, laconically. 'There's always someone who benefits from war. War is the father of all things, as Thucydides tells us.'

'And here we are in a state of war again,' said MacKenzie, the smile gone from his face. 'We have had our fair share of strife in the Highlands, as you know well, being a scholar of the civil war years, Archibald.'

'I make little progress with my History,' Stirling sighed again. 'Is there any news of Elizabeth, John?'

'Nothing, Archibald. Nothing since the sighting a couple of months ago. My clients in the north are only interested in the armies in the mountains. I've no word from her, which worries me greatly, but I'm sure Ruairidh will appear on the scene at some point. He'll put his head above the parapet, no doubt looking for money. When he does, I'll hear about it, and I'll be after him.'

'And I will help you, sir,' added Scougall, defiantly.

'Of course, thank you, Davie.' MacKenzie patted Scougall's arm. 'You're a loyal friend.' He turned back to Stirling, 'Now, there's another matter I want to discuss with you, Archibald. You'll no doubt have heard of the death of Aeneas MacLeod, son of MacLeod of Rhenigidale and foster-son of MacLeod of Dunvegan. I've been asked to investigate his death by his father. The family believe Dalrymple cares little about finding the killer. They fear he's too busy with political business.'

Stirling put down his tankard. He had a pained expression on his face and his hand sought the side of his abdomen. 'A terrible shock for the family, John. It brings a tear to my eye to think of the young writer, not much older than Davie here, slain violently and buried in an unmarked grave.' Stirling grimaced again, holding his side. 'I need to visit a physician soon.'

'Make sure you do. You look worse each time we see you.' MacKenzie waited for a few moments until the pain in Stirling's side eased, then continued. 'It's an interesting case. A vile killing, a disgraceful murder, of course. But from a purely selfish standpoint, I've agreed to help. I hope it will take my mind off Elizabeth until there's definite news. Did you know the deceased, Archibald?'

Stirling removed his hand from his side and let out a long sigh. 'I knew him not. But I've heard much about him. He was an ambitious young man and, apparently, a dedicated servant of Mrs Hair. Did you know him, Davie?'

'I did not know him well. I knew of him. I met him a couple of times. I must admit I did not take to him. But it was maybe because he was a Highlander. It was a few years ago when I had dealings with him. I now look more favourably on all things to do with the Highlands.'

'We must begin by examining the body and then visiting Mrs Hair's office,' said MacKenzie. 'What do you make of Mrs Hair, Archibald?'

'I've known her for years, although at a distance. I was an acquaintance of her first husband Robert Kennedy.' Stirling went on to explain Mrs Hair's troubled life and experiences with her two husbands. 'She was left hugely indebted at his death. Her second husband, a younger man, a druggist called Hair also died young. She has proved herself a careful business woman and amassed a considerable fortune. It's said she's now worth thousands a year, which puts her among the richest in the city. Who would have thought a woman could have achieved so much and such a diminutive one? I'm not sure how she's done it but I wish I had followed her careful management. The world of finance is a complete mystery to me. As a trader in debts she is unpopular, but she does not appear to care. She has no desire to obtain a position on the city council, even if she could get one, so she does not get bogged down in the petty intrigues required to become a councillor. She has often been seen to benefit from the misery of others.' Stirling sipped his wine and a cold smile broke on his pale face. 'I may be forced to borrow from her myself before this marriage settlement is completed. She's one of the few lenders who can still provide funds.'

MacKenzie noticed Stirling's grimace and wondered if he was in some kind of financial trouble, but before he could question his friend further about his affairs, Scougall asked: 'How has she prospered while others have failed?

'She is adept at buying and selling bonds,' replied Stirling. 'She benefits from those struggling with debt. She's often bought bonds when no others dared at very low prices, when it was thought the debtor would never repay interest or principal. She has sold the same bond at a high price when everyone sought to buy it back. She's invested in property all over the city and in surrounding estates, from which she earns rents, and uses as collateral for borrowing at low interest rates herself. She encourages her tenants to improve their lands and takes some of the higher yields. She owns estates further afield in Stirlingshire and Linlithgowshire and I've heard as far away as Glasgow. She has stakes in the American trade, and trade to the Baltic and France and Spain, with shares in vessels sailing regularly from Leith. She earns a healthy income from all these sources. Scores of men and women have borrowed from her over the years, including myself. I'll say this about her. She's strict in her terms but provides money quickly. She funds foreign trade. She funds domestic trade. She lends to lawyers and nobles and doctors and soldiers and writers. She does not base her lending on social position, rather on ability to repay. She's avoided making too many loans to the nobles who are always tardy in repayment and have been the undoing of many money men. She never provided funds for the Duke of York or King Charles. This policy has proved very wise. She's a great facilitator of trade across this nation.'

'She's a miraculous woman. Have you borrowed from her recently?' asked MacKenzie.

'No, John. I've found other sources for my present expenditure. She's one of the few moneylenders in this city I'm not indebted to, I'm sorry to say.' Stirling turned to Scougall: 'I advise you to be careful if you ever have a daughter, Davie. Do not be influenced by delusions of grandeur. Above all, stand up to your bedfellow. Seek a match for your daughter within the means of your family. Then you will have little to do with debt. A life without debt. There is a place a man could live happily! The fellow who came up with debt was no doubt Auld Nick himself!'

'It's said MacLeod leaned towards the old King,' said Scougall, hesitantly changing the subject.

'Is that such a sin?' replied Stirling, frowning, and staring down at the dregs in his tankard. 'There are many in this city and across the land, indeed across the kingdoms of Scotland, England and Ireland, who despise William and his treacherous wife, Mary, who turned against her own father. Are we all to be slain for holding such views? We did not ask for any glorious revolution. We despise it. Are we all to be persecuted? Are we all to have our throats cut and our bodies dumped in the country? Are we all to be followed everywhere by Whig dogs! Look yonder!' Stirling pointed at a cloaked figure at a table on the other side of the tavern sipping from a tankard of beer. 'That hound is on my tail. He follows me everywhere. What a waste of time and money! And who pays his wages? The government. And who pays the government? Those who pay taxes – like you and me.' Scougall felt a twinge of unease. The previous year he had suffered as a friend of the Presbyterians, now he found himself sitting among Jacobites. He despised the divisiveness of politics, the stark choice between two positions, neither of which were comfortable.

'Is there anything else you know about MacLeod that might help us, Archibald? Putting aside political issues, just viewing his death as a case of murder,' asked MacKenzie.

Stirling called for another cup of ale. 'There are still a few men who talk to me since my fall from office, but, alas, not as many as before. I no longer have money to distribute as bribes. They are less keen to give anything away for free. But some still speak to me, old acquaintances, often accidently. There's always talk in taverns, if you know where to listen, if you know who to listen to, and if you want to listen. It's an old habit of mine to pay attention. I know most of the rogues in this city who stick to the place like lichen on a rock. They may know something of MacLeod's fate – if he crossed one of them, or crossed someone else. I'll keep my ear to the ground and let you know if I hear anything.'

'What are your thoughts on Mrs Hair in relation to MacLeod's murder?'

'She's scrupulous in her business dealings,' replied Stirling. 'But many men dislike women rising so high. Do you think MacLeod was killed as a way of getting at her, as a way of damaging her interest?'

'It's possible, I suppose,' replied MacKenzie. Then his thoughts were distracted by Stirling who suddenly called out: 'Ah, here they are at last!'

Two finely-dressed women approached the table. The younger one wore a startling ruby gown. Scougall observed her close resemblance to Stirling, she was clearly his daughter. He assumed that the shorter woman next to her, also fine-looking, was Stirling's wife. Stirling appeared agitated by their appearance. He rose painfully to his feet. 'May I introduce Davie Scougall. Margaret, my wife, and Arabella, my daughter. They are in town to buy material for the wedding dress. A wedding is a never-ending expense, gentlemen! And that fool over there will no doubt follow us all the way to the tailor's shop! I'm sorry I don't have more time to help with the case, John. I wish it was different. I wish it was like the old days!'

CHAPTER 10

A Body in the Morgue

IN THE EARLY AFTERNOON MacKenzie and Scougall headed for the Tollbooth on the High Street. The Tollbooth was a sprawling mass of stone beside St Giles Kirk which acted as jail, council chamber and headquarters for the town guard. The building looked as if it had grown organically out of the road rather than designed by human agency. The morgue was in the basement, a poorly-lit, low-ceilinged, room containing a line of wooden tables. Lawtie peered up at them through thick spectacles. Scougall was always reminded of a mole emerging from its burrow. The diminutive doctor did not look pleased to see them. He was never pleased to see lawyers as he believed they looked down on him as a member of an inferior profession.

'I thought I was done with you two,' Lawtie sneered. 'But you keep popping up and it usually means trouble. I didn't expect to see you here again after your change in circumstances, Mr MacKenzie. I thought you were finished with the law and devoting your time to the garden.'

MacKenzie knew that Lawtie's tone aimed to get under his skin. Their paths had crossed often over the decades. Lawtie could not help saying everything in a snide manner. But he ignored the little barb. He had more important things to consider. 'Good day to you, Dr Lawtie. I must disappoint you, I'm not retiring to my garden yet,' he said, pushing past him into the chamber with Scougall following. Lawtie, disgruntled, closed the door behind them.

'I'm acting for MacLeod's family. They want to get to the bottom of his murder. They have doubts about the Advocate's commitment to the case, so my plants will have to wait until I've solved it.'

Lawtie sighed. 'Dalrymple has other things to worry about, as we all do. I've no time for foreign princes who seek other king's crowns. James was not a good king, indeed he was a very bad one, but he was our king. Now we're ruled by a Dutchman and crowd of rogues. I met James once, you know, when he came north as his brother's commissioner. The whole city, especially the ladies, got into a fluster about him. I took a liking for him. I cannot fathom why on earth I should. But he spent a little time talking to me, unlike you lawyers. There I've said my piece on politics. Would I take up a sword to bring James back? No, thank you. I'd not risk my pinkie for a king.'

MacKenzie reflected that Lawtie's position was close to his own, although Lawtie was perhaps an even more reluctant Jacobite. It would, of course, all be different if Dundee arrived at the gates of the city at the head of a victorious army. And what then? Bloody civil war – death and destruction. An image of the serene beauty of his gardens at the Hawthorns which he had nurtured over the years came into his mind. They might be destroyed by a marauding army; history repeating itself. The pendulum swinging back and forth: war and peace, peace and war, through the whole of history. Why was war never avoided despite the lessons of history? Was it simply that man was a beast and nothing could be done to change his nature?

Lawtie pulled back the white sheet covering the body on one of the tables. An overpowering stink rose like a wave from MacLeod's cadaver. Scougall covered his nose and turned away in disgust. The putrefying body was not like others he had seen. It was not a freshly-killed corpse, but a rotting pile of decaying flesh. Placing a handkerchief over his face, MacKenzie moved closer to examine it.

'He's already in a state of some putrefaction, as you can smell, gentlemen. I'd judge he lay under the earth for a couple of weeks at least,' said Lawtie, resting a hand territorially on the corpse, and seeming to enjoy their reaction to the smell.

MacKenzie observed everything carefully. His eyes took a few moments to adapt to the camouflage of decay on the body. He could make out breeches, jacket, boots, belt, cloak, and periwig – the clothes of a lawyer, not a Highland man. The face was partly decomposed, but the features were still visible.

'How did he die in your opinion, Dr Lawtie?' asked MacKenzie, taking a couple of paces back from the body.

'His throat was cut. It's obvious enough. There's no doubt about the cause of death, MacKenzie.' Lawtie pointed to a black gash across the neck. It was difficult to see at first, amongst the decaying flesh. 'There must've been huge blood loss. Death followed in seconds.' MacKenzie took an old glove from his pocket. Putting it on, he moved MacLeod's head to the side to observe the wound across the neck.

'A quick death,' Lawtie continued. 'Perhaps, a death we might all wish for. Like the beast in the slaughter house, little time to ponder the mystery of life or the pain of Hell in his last moments, little time to fear the eternal flames!'

'What kind of weapon was used?' asked Scougall, trying to appear useful, but still disgusted by the overpowering odour.

'I would judge a dirk of about this length.' Lawtie indicated with his hands a blade of six inches. 'It was wielded swiftly and skilfully. There's also another minor wound on the back of the head. He was possibly struck first with a blunt implement, probably made unconscious, before being killed, before his neck was slashed. He's all yours, gentlemen. Do with him as you will.'

Lawtie withdrew to his desk at the side of the room. He sat down and began to write in a ledger. MacKenzie continued to observe the corpse and, after circling the table a few times, kneeled down on the floor to observe the wound on the back of the head. Scougall hung back, his thoughts bleak: Why would God allow such decay from a creature made in his own image? He was recalling the killings of the previous year and his own close shave with death. He had an overwhelming desire to get out of the room but did not want to appear feeble in front of MacKenzie, or, for that matter, Lawtie. He forced himself to wander round the table, looking at the body from different angles, beginning to feel nauseous. He could not get used to the idea of the body's decay. His thoughts strayed to MacLeod's soul, now evaporated from his cadaver. Had his soul gone to Heaven or Hell? A vision of the young lawyer amongst the flames of Hell, screaming in agony, flashed through his mind. Where was he, Scougall himself, bound after death? He was also a sinner, but he was surely promised eternal bliss? Was he one of the Lord's Elect? He had not done much bad in the world, he hoped. But, he reflected, he had not done much good either. He was startled out of his reverie by MacKenzie shouting across the room: 'Was there anything else you found on him, Lawtie?'

'I checked through all the pockets in his trousers and jacket,' Lawtie replied, looking up from his ledger. 'There was nothing else on him. Do you have any thoughts on the motive of the murderer? Theft?'

'You're sure there was nothing?' MacKenzie asked again, ignoring Lawtie's question.

'Not a thing. I checked everywhere. Look for yourself. Do you take me for a fool MacKenzie?' Lawtie replied angrily.

MacKenzie turned to Scougall. 'Turn out your pockets, Davie. On the table, there.'

'What?' Scougall did not understand his request.

'Turn out your pockets. There on the table.' MacKenzie indicated the table next to MacLeod's body. Scougall rummaged in his pockets and placed everything on the table. The small pile included a comb, a few coins, a number of letters and papers, a few pencils, a quill, a small tinder box and a candle stub.

'The pockets of an Edinburgh writer tell us much about his profession,' said MacKenzie. 'There are at least a dozen items here and Davie is a tidy man. But MacLeod had nothing in his. What can you conclude from this, Davie?'

'I don't know, sir. That he had emptied them before he was killed?'

MacKenzie shook his head. 'More likely they were emptied after he was killed, either by the killer or the person who found the body. And look here.' Scougall was forced to get close to the body as MacKenzie pulled back MacLeod's jacket, raised a hem and inserted two fingers. 'A secret pocket, useful for a lawyer or someone involved in political activity. But nothing in here either. We have little to be going on. We only know it was a brutal death. Someone took everything that was on him.' He glanced up at his assistant. 'We need to learn more about the character of Aeneas MacLeod. Let's start with Mrs Hair.'

CHAPTER 11

Mrs Hair's Office

MACKENZIE AND SCOUGALL left the morgue and made straight for MacPherson's Land across the High Street from the Tollbooth. Mrs Hair's office on the first floor was reached through a warren of small rooms and passageways, some rented to artisans, merchants and writers, others crammed with writers working for her. Scougall estimated she must employ twenty people. It was a considerable concern, the house of Hair – it must be one of the largest in Edinburgh. Galbraith showed them into her chamber. Scougall was intrigued to observe her business first hand. He had heard so much about her, but had never visited her premises, and was surprised by her small, Spartan office. It was a plainly decorated room with a desk, a few chairs and a wooden press. He had expected one of the wealthiest moneylenders in the city to have something grander.

'Take a seat please, gentleman.' Mrs Hair indicated they should sit on the two chairs in front of her desk. They were little more than stools. Scougall felt like he was sitting on a child's chair. MacKenzie, who was a tall man, looked ridiculous perched on his. Scougall watched Mrs Hair's thin, rat-like face as she sat behind her large desk. She had tiny, darting eyes behind round spectacles. Her eyes burned with life, alert, observing everything.

MacKenzie took in his surroundings as Mrs Hair tidied away some papers into a drawer. The room, from his perspective, was calm and serene. The only items on the desk were a quill and ink stand, and a large leather-bound ledger which was closed and on which she rested a territorial arm.

What was recorded in it obviously meant a great deal to her. MacKenzie noticed two portraits on one wall, each depicting a middle-aged man dressed soberly in black. They were probably her husbands, he thought. On the wall facing her desk was a landscape of a house and gardens with hills in the background.

'Can I provide you with some refreshments, gentlemen?' she asked in a friendly manner.

'We are fine, Mrs Hair. Thank you. Let me get straight to the point, if I may.' MacKenzie smiled warmly. 'You know MacLeod's body was found at Craigleith Quarry?'

Mrs Hair sighed and turned to look out the window. 'Indeed, Mr MacKenzie. He was a promising young man, most exact in all his work in the office. He was a writer of exemplary style, destined for great things in business. We were, of course, very worried when he disappeared without word. We reported it to the authorities and made our own search for him around the city and sent word to his father in the Highlands, in case he had travelled home. What on earth do you think happened to him, Mr MacKenzie?'

'That is what we intend to find out, madam. Let me explain. I'm acting for his father, MacLeod of Rhenigidale, who is travelling to Edinburgh as we speak to retrieve his son's body for burial. MacLeod of Dunvegan himself, Aeneas's foster father, wants to get to the bottom of the murder. They've lost a promising agent of the clan, an important cog in the machine. They view his killing as a direct attack on the clan MacLeod.'

'Was he murdered?' she asked. 'I've heard rumours on the street suggesting he was.'

'We must suppose he was, madam, until evidence suggests otherwise – unless he slashed his own throat and arranged for someone to throw his body in a pit.'

Mrs Hair closed her eyes. 'It's so terrible I can barely think about it. He was so... full of life and so young... a promising young man, a true Highlander...'

'I'm sorry, madam. I must be blunt in what I say. But a murder is no time for niceties. We must call a spade a spade, if we're to get to the bottom of it.'

'It's all right, Mr MacKenzie. I'm not squeamish. I've seen many terrible things in my life. It's a dreadful loss for his family. It's also a loss for the office of Hair. Of course, my loss is tiny compared to his clan's.'

'I want to ask you a few questions about him, madam. We need to build up a picture of him. It will help us find his killer and hopefully determine why he was killed. Mr Scougall, my assistant, will take notes in shorthand, if that's all right with you.'

Mrs Hair nodded approvingly at Scougall. 'A most useful skill for a notary.'

Scougall gave her a nervous smile. He felt strangely fearful before this diminutive woman. She looked small, wrinkled and ancient. But she ruled over a prosperous business empire. She was more successful than most merchants in the city and they did not like her for it. He knew rumours circulated about her: she had poisoned her husbands, she had killed her children, she was a witch who used magic to divine the future. Thus, she was always on the right side of a transaction. She was the only buyer of property during the stop in affairs when news of William's landing in Torbay reached the city and prices dropped like a stone. She was the sole buyer and prices rebounded quickly. How could it be right that God rewarded her in this sphere of life while turning against her natural role as mother?

Mrs Hair sat forward on her chair, straightened her back and brought her tiny hands together as if in prayer. Removing her spectacles, she folded them and put them down on the desk. 'Let me see. I first heard about Mr MacLeod from the notary Alexander Carmichael. He recommended him to me. Carmichael has worked for me on and off for twenty years. I often seek him out when I require a writer. It was about three years ago. I'm always looking for talented writers with an eye for business.' She turned to Scougall as she said this. He wondered if her office would be a good place to work. 'He told me he wished to gain experience of the world of trade, so he could serve his clan in the future,' she continued. 'I took him on in that capacity. I had my own reasons for recruiting a

Highlander. I believed some connection might do my business good. I've little knowledge of the Highlands and no influence there. I'm a Lowlander through and through. I anticipated there would be plenty of business to be done with the chiefs. Their finances were in disarray. There would be need of order in the management of their debts. Many chiefs are dragged down by financial woes. You can buy their bonds at a very low price – as low as a few pence in the pound. Why should they be so cheap? I keep asking myself. Does the price reflect their true value? I thought there might be good business to do with the chiefs. MacLeod was a way into this new business for the House of Hair. And I am pleased to say he helped me complete a few transactions with Highlanders which delivered a good profit. Other deals are left to be completed.' She tapped the ledger on her desk, almost affectionately.

'Was he reliable?' asked MacKenzie, adjusting his position painfully on the tiny chair.

'He was, certainly, in matters relating to work. He was early at his desk and often still there when I left the office. He was conscientious and precise in all the writing he did for me. He had a good hand and a sharp eye. As I've said, he advised me wisely about the financial condition of certain chiefs: the quality of their lands and how likely they were to pay interest and principal. I had little to reprimand him for… in his work, that is.'

'But you had reason to reprimand him for something else?' MacKenzie probed.

'I must be honest with you, gentlemen. After all, we are concerned with his murder. He was keen to promote his own business interests outside my office. I was happy for him to do so, as long as he worked hard for me. It does a man no good to be suffocated by his daily work. It makes him unhappy and rebellious and he will soon leave as your enemy – the years he was employed in the office would be wasted. A busy man delivers much more than a frustrated one, who will only hate his imprisonment. I had nothing to complain about his legal work.'

'What complaints were there about him then, madam?' repeated MacKenzie.

Mrs Hair hesitated for a moment, as if she was looking for the right words. 'One was the kind I have dealt with often in this office. It came from one of the office lasses. MacLeod had eyes upon her. She's a bonnie thing. She refused his advances. It was settled with little disruption to the office.'

'She left your employ?' asked Scougall, looking up from his notebook.

Mrs Hair gave him a sharp look. 'Of course not, Mr Scougall. She remained in my employ. I warned MacLeod his behaviour was unacceptable. If he persisted, if he continued to pester her, if he tried to put his hands on her again, I would get rid of him. He took the warning seriously and stopped pestering her. She still works here.'

'What is her name?' asked MacKenzie.

'Betty McGrain. She's a good girl. She manages the affairs of the office. She makes sure everything is in order, paper and quills ordered, the place kept clean and tidy, the kitchen well stocked with victuals. I've great hopes for her in the future.'

'And the other incident you referred to?' She hesitated again. MacKenzie saw she was cautious in everything she said, weighing up what she was about to say, as if pondering a financial transaction.

'The other incident was of a rather different nature,' she answered. 'It was a more serious one. It was a sensitive matter at a time when everything was up in the air, politically. It came to my attention that MacLeod held mocking views towards King William. Reflecting this stance, he had produced certain etchings. I believe they were drawn by him in the office during moments of leisure. These crude pieces of art circulated around the chambers, from floor to floor, causing hilarity or great offence, depending on the leanings of the viewer. You see, gentlemen, folk on both sides of the political divide work in my office.'

'What were they of, madam?' Observing her, MacKenzie was sure he detected a slight smile on Mrs Hair's serious face.

'They were caricatures of some of our politicians, in particular those associated with the Presbyterian faction of the government. Men like the Chancellor and the Advocate.'

'Are you saying MacLeod was a Jacobite, Mrs Hair?' asked Scougall.

'I'm saying no such thing. I'm only saying he drew etchings of the Chancellor and the Advocate. I was quite clear with him on this point, when I found out there had been a stir in the office. His politics was his own business. If someone asked me about my own position, I would say I veered more to the side of William, but I have done good business under King James and his brother Charles. I am first and foremost a business woman. I'm not committed in the political sphere, unlike other merchants in the city who despise the old King. I know some in my office favour the old and some the new. I must be careful at a time of such disagreement across the nation. I need to make sure that whatever way the wind blows, my business will not suffer too much. One writer in the office, however, was incensed by MacLeod's etchings. He came from the opposing faction to MacLeod. He was a supporter of William and Mary and a great hater of the old King. He despised James and was not reticent at expressing his views, no doubt to the annoyance of those who supported the other party, like MacLeod. He took great offence at the etchings as insulting to the men who formed William's government. There was a fracas in the office. He left my employ by his own volition shortly after the incident, decrying my house as one that favoured Jacobites, and making a lot of noise about it all, screaming and shouting on his way down the street. I believe I am well rid of him. He now struggles on his own account as a solitary writer in a booth. He's perhaps just a young fool, I wish him no ill will, but he was too much of the fanatic to make a career in the House of Hair.'

'Did you keep the etchings by any chance, madam?' asked MacKenzie.

She rose from her seat and crossed the room. Scougall saw she was about the height of his own mother. He was reminded of a nimble bird moving across the chamber, a thin wiry thing dressed in an old-fashioned black frock, slightly stooped, no doubt caused by years at a desk. She removed some papers from a press and handed them to MacKenzie who had taken the opportunity to change his position again on the uncomfortable stool.

'Scurrilous nonsense,' she said. 'Keep them if you like. I don't know why I still have them. Although I must admit MacLeod did have a modicum of artistic talent, though not much. There is humour in them. There is no doubt about that. They hit the nail on the head.'

MacKenzie looked down at a caricature of King William with his breeches round his ankles, revealing enormous flabby buttocks from which he defecated onto a map of Scotland, under the title 'Our New King Loves the Scottish Nation'. He could not help smirking as he handed it to Scougall. The second one was of a group of men, clearly members of the government, a couple of individuals could be identified by characteristics of dress, being driven into the flames of Hell by the Devil. A Latin caption suggested they had taken bribes and sold Scotland down the river. MacKenzie chuckled. Scougall, coming from the opposing political faction, did not see the funny side, but refrained from commenting. MacLeod was an ardent Jacobite, he thought, a follower of the Whore of Babylon. He could expect nothing good from such a man. He said nothing of this to MacKenzie, however.

'What was the name of the man who left the office?' asked MacKenzie when Mrs Hair had returned to her desk.

'Adam Scobie,' Mrs Hair answered. 'He hails from Ayrshire in the western shires. His family are deep in the Covenanting fold. Some were followers of the fanatic preacher Renwick who challenged the authority of any King. His relatives swarmed into Edinburgh to hasten the end of King James – a lot of fanatics, as far as I'm concerned. He rents a chamber in Niven's Close and now earns his living by serving Presbyterian clients, a species not known for generosity when paying fees.'

'What exactly happened between MacLeod and Scobie, Mrs Hair?'

'It was all foolishness. MacLeod showed the etchings around the office. They passed from desk to desk, accompanied by bellows of laughter. Scobie was disgusted. In full hearing of everyone, he decried MacLeod as a Papist-loving dog, an inveterate Jacobite and other terms of abuse. It might have gone no further, but he launched an attack on him. They were soon brawling on the floor of the office like a couple of curs. They had to be restrained by colleagues. That was not the end of the business. Another argument broke out in a tavern later. More kicks and punches and threats. There was talk of a duel and other such nonsense. I was ready to get rid of Scobie as everyone told me he landed the first punch, but he saved me the trouble. He resigned the next day, saying he could no longer work in a den of iniquity and other overblown nonsense. I did nothing to keep him. I saw his continued presence would be toxic to the smooth running of the office. I try to encourage a modicum of tolerance, gentlemen. Scobie has struck out on his own, working from the Luckenbooths. He must be struggling to make ends meet.' She did not look particularly concerned by this. It was as if such troubles were a normal part of business.

'Do you think he could have killed MacLeod?' proposed Scougall, hesitantly. He had learned first-hand how the fanaticism of some Presbyterians might drive them to commit atrocious acts.

'I don't think so, but it's possible,' she replied. 'He had a volatile character. He was very quick to anger. His passions inflamed by ministers of the Presbyterian persuasion who thunder from their pulpits every Sabbath against the Whore of Babylon. But would he kill MacLeod? In my opinion, I think it unlikely.'

'Can you think of anyone else who might want to kill him? Could Betty McGrain have been driven by revenge?' asked MacKenzie.

Mrs Hair shook her head. 'No. There was no debauch of the lass. She's a gentle creature. I believe MacLeod left her alone after I had words with him. Why would she risk so much?'

'You mentioned MacLeod's other business interests. Could you tell us what they were?'

'I was aware of some of them. He was following the path I've taken in business. Money is best made from money and borrowing is always in fashion, those are the two maxims I hold. I knew MacLeod was lending money on his own account, building up a book of debt, as we call it. I've been told he also bought and sold goods, importing them from abroad. That was his business, as far as I was concerned. I've heard he dealt in those goods favoured by the Highland gentry. You will know what I mean, Mr MacKenzie. Items such as tapestries and paintings and furniture and books, indeed all the luxuries which flood into the Highlands, which the chiefs and gentry cannot afford and which they must borrow to pay for, mostly from Edinburgh lawyers and merchants. He also advised clients in Edinburgh and in the Highlands, no doubt mostly members of his clan. He was often seen with Highlanders in taverns, although, of course, I don't frequent such places, as a respectable woman. I hear that he did. Like you, Mr MacKenzie, MacLeod was prone to complete deals in the Irish tongue. Such is the nature of good business, gentleman. Diversify your interests, diversify your interests. At some point his work for me would have become burdensome to him. Then he would've left my establishment to establish his own. Then, I may have offered to share an interest or two with him, perhaps in a boat to the Caribbean or a consignment of furniture for a castle in the Highlands. I've done so with other talented men who've left my office to establish their own concerns. They maintain good relations with me, rather than competing against me. I'm sure he would've been successful and looked after his father's concerns and that of his chief. I hoped he would have continued to provide me advice on the finances of other chiefs.'

'Do you think his politics had anything to do with his death?' asked Scougall.

'It's possible... politics is often a man's... undoing. In my opinion, he was too attached to the cause of the old King.

But who can look inside another's heart and know what they have suffered. Supporting the old King might be construed as running counter to sound business sense. We must see which way the wind blows, Mr Scougall.'

'Were there any others who did not look kindly on him in the office?' asked MacKenzie.

'I'm sure there are many. He liked to provoke a reaction in folk. You must ask around yourselves. They will know more about it than me. Men like MacLeod always make enemies among their contemporaries. He was loquacious. He had the gift of the gab. He told jokes at others' expense. All feigned to like him to his face, because they were scared his sharp tongue might be turned on them. With me, he was all politeness, but I'm sure he mocked me behind my back. It's the usual way of the creature called man.'

MacKenzie smiled. 'You are an observant student of the male sex, madam. Do you yourself have any particular enemies?'

She hesitated for a moment, removing her spectacles again and placing them carefully on the desk. 'What exactly do you mean, Mr MacKenzie?'

'Could MacLeod have been killed as a way of getting at you? As a way of damaging your interest? Were there any particular transactions he was helping you with at the time of his death?'

Mrs Hair's face broke into a smile. 'He was only a junior writer in my office, Mr MacKenzie. He was hardly a vital cog in the Hair empire. Regarding my enemies in this city, where can I start? How many pages do you have in your notebook, Mr Scougall! During every one of the last twenty years I've been in business, I've faced men who have cursed me, who have tried to rob me and who despised me just because of my sex. So, go and stop any merchant on the High Street and ask them what they think of old Mrs Hair, or Mary Erskine, as some still call me, and, if they answer truthfully, they'll say they despise me as a disgrace to my sex. All the men in this city are my enemies, every last one of them. Every man in Edinburgh!' She squealed in laughter. 'But killing MacLeod to get at me? I don't think so. I cared little for him, really.'

'I understand, Mrs Hair. You are unusual in this day. You are a successful, independent woman,' said MacKenzie, moving forward on the uncomfortable stool. 'But of the hundreds of rogues who go by the name of merchant or writer or anything else in this city, are there any who bear a particular grudge against you?'

'Let me think. Legal cases over the years, money lent and not repaid, properties seized from bankrupts. Many are unhappy with me. I would not know where to start – doctors, merchants, lawyers, nobles, soldiers, ministers. A few have tried to destroy me over the years! Most of them are now dead. I've had to live by my wits!'

'Are you willing to provide any names?'

'There are so many, gentlemen, so many. Start with the council of this city, all of them, then the merchant guilds. If you forced me to name a few candidates, I might suggest the names Dunlop, Slight and Cant. Dunlop and Slight are dead. Cant is decrepit and bed-ridden. And before you ask, I did not have any of them blown up in the Canongate! I've simply outlived them all. The younger generation are not so difficult to deal with. They have a little respect for me.'

'If anyone else comes to mind, please let us know.' MacKenzie felt that she was not telling them all she knew.

'I'll inform you of course, Mr MacKenzie. Let me ponder the matter more deeply.'

'Is there anything else you can tell us about MacLeod? The places he frequented, particular associates, anything that might be useful. Anything he was working on before he died.'

'I believe he was often a customer in the Targe Tavern and establishments like Gourlay's and Maggie Lister's. Of his associates, I'm not entirely sure. I think the lawyer David Drummond was a close friend. At the time of his death he was preparing instruments for the purchase of Henderson's Land and working on a series of transactions concerned with debts of the Earl of Dewarton. He was also advising me on the purchase of a small bundle of debts on the estate of Fraser of Lovat.

Apart from that, there's little else to say. Is it not likely he was robbed and killed for a few pounds?'

'It's possible, madam. We just do not know why he was killed. But one way or the other, we'll find out. I've just one last question, not directly related to MacLeod. The recent explosion in the Canongate which killed Dunlop and Slight and others. What do you make of it?

She sighed again. 'Why would a merchant store powder under his own house? It is madness. It's a complete mystery to me.'

'And now the tenement is up for sale?'

'It will cost a small fortune to rebuild after such devastation.'

'Will you be a bidder for it?'

She did not reply immediately, but placed the palm of her hand on the ledger and gave it a gentle tap. Her face opened into a broad smile. 'I expect I will be, depending on the price, of course. Property is a good asset, gentlemen. It's the best you can own, especially Edinburgh property.'

'You would be a beneficiary of a terrible explosion!' spluttered Scougall, then immediately regretted what he had said. His face turned crimson and he dropped his eyes back on his shorthand.

Mrs Hair's chirpy demeanour disappeared. 'I would rebuild the tenement with my own money, Mr Scougall. The city would benefit from that. Surely you cannot be insinuating I was involved in such a thing? An old maid like me a conspirator in a powder plot! You do amuse me, sir.' Scougall wanted the floor to eat him up.

'Mr Scougall did not want to suggest that, madam. I'm sure. What is your opinion of the explosion?'

'No sane merchant would store powder under his own residence.'

'So, it was placed there by another?'

'I would say that is the most likely explanation.'

MacKenzie rose stiffly to his feet. 'Thank you for answering our questions. With your permission, might we examine MacLeod's desk and speak to others in your office?'

'If you insist. Mr Galbraith will show you round. I believe there's nothing of interest in the desk. Galbraith has examined the instrument book already. Everything appeared to be in order. Everything was up to date. It was as if MacLeod knew he would be leaving. Perhaps he planned to do so. His instrument book is still on his desk.'

'May Mr Scougall peruse it? Just in case something has been missed? He has a keen eye.'

'I grant you permission. Please inform me if you find anything. I must seek out the services of another writer for my office. I would prefer one with Highland contacts, if possible. Perhaps you, or Mr Scougall, can recommend somebody?'

Scougall wondered again if his own interests would be served by working in Mrs Hair's office. She could teach him a thing or two about money and trade. It would be a change from the dry business of the notary public. Foreign trade interested him, particularly. He longed to see foreign shores like the West Indies. When the case was over, he might seek a meeting with her to discuss the opening. He hoped, slightly nervously, that his previous comment had not damaged his chances.

As they rose to leave, MacKenzie pointed to the landscape painting. 'What is the picture of, madam?' She got up from behind the desk and came over to stand under it.

'Garlet House in Clackmannanshire with the Ochil Hills beyond. It's where I was born many, many years ago! I return when I can, when I want to get out of the city, when I'm fed up with the world of business. It's a place where I can clear my head. It's full of happy memories of my childhood. It's where I lived before I married Mr Kennedy.' She was lost in thought for a few moments, staring intently at the painting. She turned to point at one of the portraits on the other wall. 'That's him. He died in 1671, leaving me a poor relict, a poor relict with nothing in my kist but sad memories and a pile of debt. I learned a lot about business from him. I learned what I should not do. I still think of him each time I sign a deed. What would Mr Kennedy do, I ask myself? If the answer is sign, I do not do it! I married Mr Hair a few years later. He was my choice, not my father's. He served me well, at least that's what they say on the street, is it not, gentlemen?' She smiled, beckoning them with outstretched arms to leave. 'I'm a simple soul, really. I do business for myself and for those who serve me. I regard the loyal ones who stay more than a couple of years as my family. I hope by my business to leave the world a little better than when I entered it, especially the poor sex of women who suffer so much in this world at the hands of men.' She turned to Scougall who was embarrassed to feel her gaze upon him: 'I do hope it's not the same order of things in the next world, Mr Scougall!'

Galbraith showed them into a small chamber at the back of the tenement just down the corridor from Mrs Hair's office. It was plainly decorated with wood panels and contained two small desks, back to back. Galbraith remained at the door, while MacKenzie and Scougall entered.

'What was your impression of Mr MacLeod, Mr Galbraith?' MacKenzie asked him.

'He was friendly enough, sir. He worked hard. He could be a bit arrogant. He had no time for fools like me. He was quick of tongue. I usually let him be. I laughed at his jokes. He was younger than me anyway. He was ambitious. I'm happy to serve Mrs Hair.' Galbraith had a lugubrious, staccato way of speaking in short sentences.

'What do you mean, Mr Galbraith?' asked MacKenzie.

'I mean his tongue could be sharp, if you got on the wrong side of him. He regarded himself as a cut above the rest of us. I don't know why it should be. Perhaps it was his upbringing in the household of a chief. He kept going on about how he was the foster-son of MacLeod of Dunvegan. He never stopped telling you that. You would see him in the tavern or the coffee house speaking away in Irish with his cronies, looking quite the man about town, quite the dandy, lording it over everyone. God knows what he said about us all!'

MacKenzie smiled and said something in Gaelic which only he understood. Galbraith returned the smile sheepishly. MacKenzie looked through the sash window onto the black stone of the tenement behind. He suddenly felt annoyed. They were making little progress in the case. His mood darkened. From the time his own father had died when he was a child he had experienced sudden shifts of mood. They were like the appearance of dark clouds on a summer's day. His face would suddenly assume a brutal seriousness, causing consternation in some and fear in others, as if he had taken grim offence at their very existence. This natural predilection he had used to his advantage in his chosen profession of advocate, lulling those he questioned in court into a false sense of security with his affability before glowering down at them like a demented minister. It was a tactic which could disarm an opponent and encourage them to say things they did not intend. When he turned back to Galbraith, the expression of playfulness was gone from his face. 'Why do you think he was killed?' he asked sternly.

Galbraith was surprised by the abrupt question and the change of expression on MacKenzie's face. 'It wasn't me, sir!' he exclaimed defensively.

'I didn't suggest it was you, Mr Galbraith,' MacKenzie replied bluntly.

'If you ask me, I think he was mixed up with some stuff. I'm sure he was mixed up with something bad. I've seen him in conversation with...' Galbraith did not finish the sentence.

'In conversation with whom exactly?' asked MacKenzie.

Galbraith looked behind him to make sure there was no one in the corridor. His voice dropped to a whisper. 'George Gourlay and Captain Stein. Why would he be speaking with the likes of them? Why would a lawyer want anything to do with them?'

'Why indeed?'

'They are the kind of men I avoid in a tavern. They have a reputation for getting what they want from people. MacLeod appeared to seek out that kind, to court the company of men who would be described as criminals. I don't know why Mrs Hair had anything to do with him.'

'You would describe the Captain of the Guard as a criminal, Mr Galbraith?'

'It's only what I've heard about him. He's a man who leans on people, but I've never spoken to him myself.'

'Why would MacLeod have anything to do with these men?' asked Scougall who had grown used to MacKenzie's sudden shifts of tone. He could sense that Galbraith was uncomfortable to be questioned.

'I don't know. It was said he had business dealings with them. But the nature of the business, I don't know.'

MacKenzie moved closer to Galbraith, emphasising his height over him. Galbraith tried to back off into the corridor. 'What about MacLeod's relations with Scobie?'

Galbarith continued to reply in a terrified whisper. 'Scobie was a young fool. He was lazy. He was slow. He was prone to making stupid mistakes. He blamed others. MacLeod considered him an oaf. He was always the butt of his jokes. Scobie took offence at some stupid drawings. I believe it was just an excuse for attacking MacLeod, for getting back at his cutting comments about Presbyterians. They brawled in the office and again in a tavern. It began to get serious. Scobie challenged him to a duel. MacLeod just laughed it off.'

'Do you think Scobie could have killed him?'

Galbraith looked away. 'I don't think so, sir. Scobie is quick to anger but I believe he has a good Christian soul.'

'Why do you say that?'

'I've seen him in the kirk on the Sabbath. I've seen him praying. I've watched him in the pew in front of me praying with all his heart, beseeching his Maker, fervently. I've seen the expression on his face as he prays. He's a fool, but no killer. Scobie is a God-fearing man.'

MacKenzie turned on his heels and wandered back into the room to look out the window. When he turned back to Galbraith his tone changed again. The storm had passed. 'Who uses the other desk?' he asked affably.

Galbraith appeared to relax. He came forward himself into the chamber. 'Farquharson, a junior writer, an apprentice in the office. MacLeod was overseeing his work for a few months. He was given to different writers to spread the burden of teaching.'

'Where is he now?'

'He's been transferred to another room, now that MacLeod is gone.'

'Thank you, Mr Galbraith. That's all, for now. I may want to speak with you again,' said MacKenzie smiling.

When Galbraith had disappeared down the corridor, MacKenzie shut the door behind him. He looked around the sparse interior. There was little of anything remarkable in the office. A lawyer's writing chamber like any other. Two desks and two chairs, barely room to swing a rabbit.

Scougall stood sheepishly at the window. 'What do you make of Mrs Hair, Davie?' MacKenzie asked, lowering his voice to a whisper.

Scougall chose his words carefully. For some reason he felt that he had to speak well of her in her own premises. 'She appears to be a remarkable woman,' was all he could think of saying.

'We must find out who her enemies are.' MacKenzie paced around slowly deep in thought. He remembered MacLeod's instrument book on the desk. 'I'll leave you here, Davie. Note anything of interest you find. We might not get the opportunity again. Then, seek out Betty McGrain. I'm going to visit MacLeod's lodgings.'

Scougall spent a dull couple of hours in MacLeod's chamber reading his instrument book that recorded his legal work. He made a series of notes about recent transactions itemised and then spoke to the other writers in the offices off the corridor. They all provided a similar picture of MacLeod. He was a cocky Highland lawyer. He was then directed by Galbraith to the basement where he found Betty McGrain in a small chamber off the kitchen. She was writing in a ledger, deep in concentration, and startled when he put his head round the door.

'Are you Miss McGrain?' Scougall asked hesitantly. He was uncomfortable interviewing young women.

'You gave me a fright, sir! Who are you?' She looked perturbed by his appearance, as if she had remembered something unpleasant.

'My name's Scougall, Davie Scougall. I'm a notary. I've a chamber of my own just up the High Street.'

'That's very good, Mr Scougall,' she said in a faltering voice. 'But you've taken a wrong turn. The writers are all on the first floor.'

'I've been there already, thank you. It's you I'm looking for, Miss McGrain. I've been directed here by Mr Galbraith. I'm sorry to bother you. I can see you're busy.' Scougall moved into the small room and stood opposite her. She was a small woman of about twenty years, bonnie enough, he thought. He did not know if he should take the chair opposite her at the table. Would it be too forward? He decided to remain standing. 'I'm working with the advocate John MacKenzie. We're investigating the killing of a man who used to work in this office. Aeneas MacLeod.'

At the mention of the name, she put down her pen and straightened her back. Her face grew dark and she closed her eyes for a moment.

'We've spoken to Mrs Hair already. She's told us, how can I put this, that MacLeod was someone… who was known to you.' Scougall was looking for the right words which did not come easily. He began to splutter nervously. 'That he was… that he was…'

'I had no time for the likes of him!' she replied angrily, her reticence disappearing. 'What right did he have to put his hands on me? Just because I'm only a maid in this office? Why did he presume he had rights over me? Thank God I work in an establishment run by an honourable woman like Mrs Hair. If it had been the office of a man, I would've been cast out on the street.'

Scougall found himself on the defensive after her outburst. 'I'm sorry, Miss McGrain. Please forgive me. I'm sure it's difficult for you to talk about him. We're just trying to find out what happened. MacLeod's family want to know why he

was killed. Do you know... do you know anything about it?'
Scougall winced at the choice of his own words.

She closed the book and looked up at him. There was anger
in her eyes. 'I'm sorry he's dead, sir. It's terrible for anyone to
have their throat cut and be buried alone without family in
attendance. But I'm glad he does not work in the office any
more. I prefer it here now he's dead. He can abuse me no longer.'

Scougall nodded knowingly. 'Could you describe him to
me, Miss McGrain?'

'Why do you need me to describe him?'

'Mr MacKenzie told me to ask you these questions.'
Scougall was struggling for the right words. He felt his cheeks
warm. He would be glad when the interview was over. He
preferred it when MacKenzie asked the questions and he noted
down the answers. 'Mr MacKenzie is most exact in all he does
in such cases. He demands to know as much as possible about
the victim. In this way, we'll be able to find out the identity of
the killer and the reason for the killing. Every little detail might
be important to us. On its own, a single fact may appear trivial,
but when combined with others, a fuller picture emerges. The
picture comes into focus like light through a lens.' Scougall was
trying to remember exactly how MacKenzie had put it to him
many times over the years they had worked together.

She crossed her hands over her chest, defensively. 'I don't
like even thinking about him.'

'It's very important that justice is done – in the eyes of God.'
Scougall tried to smile to put her at ease.

She gave a nervous smile in return. She had realised that
he was more nervous than her. 'Very well, Mr Scougall. If you
insist, I'll tell you what I know about him.' She closed the book
and sat back in her chair. 'He was nice enough to me to begin
with. He was friendly enough. He chatted away about this and
that. He told me about his home in the Highlands and what
it was like being fostered by a chief and living in Dunvegan
Castle. I thought we got on well. I thought we were friends.' She
paused for a moment gathering her thoughts.

'Then what happened?' asked Scougall, looking up from his notebook. He was recording every word carefully.

'Then things suddenly changed. One evening I was tidying up in his office. I thought everyone had gone home for the night when suddenly I felt a presence behind me. There was the sound of footsteps, then the smell of wine. Before I could turn, a man was feeling me, squeezing me, pushing me against the wall.'

Scougall looked up again. He could not hide the expression of disgust on his face. 'What did you do?'

'I managed to get loose somehow. When I was able to turn at last, I was shocked to see it was him. I tried to strike him on the face. But he grabbed my wrist tightly, painfully. He said, swaying with the drink, something like: "I'll have you soon enough Betty McGrain, be sure of it, I'll have you. I'll have you over my desk here. You'll beg me for it. I'll take you here soon enough."' She stopped for a few moments, closing her eyes and breathing out. 'There, I did not want to say it,' she continued. 'But that's what he said. And he spewed out other things with his wine-breath in the Irish tongue in a lascivious way.'

'How did you get away from him?'

'I ran away to the kitchen to get a knife but he didn't follow me. I escaped out the back door and went home. I cried all night. I dreaded going back to the office the next day, but it was as if nothing had happened. It was as if he had forgotten it ever happened. Perhaps he had. He was very drunk, I said to myself. Perhaps it will never happen again. Perhaps it was a one-off. Perhaps he's not a bad sort.' She looked Scougall straight in the eye. He was struck by their piercing blue colour.

'For a few weeks I saw little of him,' she continued. 'He didn't seek me out and things settled down again as I went about my business. I was happy enough. I'd almost forgotten about the incident. Then one night I was making my way home through Jake's Vennel. It was in the gloaming. You know, it's a dark narrow passageway when the sun sets behind St Giles. As I was about to come out onto the High Street, someone grabbed me from the shadows. I thought I was going to be robbed. I tried to scream but a hand was thrust over my mouth.

A face came up close to mine, stinking of liquor. I realised it was him again. This time he was more forceful. He took me by the throat. I could hardly breathe. He said if I did not treat him kindly in the office he would take me by force anyway. He swore at me and said many hateful things. He stood looking at me for a minute or so, still holding my throat, before staggering off drunkenly. I caught my breath and ran home, locking my door. I was terrified. I could not sleep a wink all night. It is painful for me to recall it.'

'Just take your time, Miss McGrain,' said Scougall, appalled by the picture she was painting of MacLeod. The man surely deserved to die if he prayed on women in this manner.

'The next morning, I summoned up the courage to speak to Mrs Hair. I told her everything that had happened. She listened attentively to me. She said I was not to worry. She would speak with him. I didn't stay late in the office on my own after that. I made sure there were always folk about. For a long while, perhaps a couple of months, I had no bother from him. He didn't come down to the basement, as he had done before. He sent one of the boys for drink or victuals and hardly looked at me when I had some business in the writers' chambers. I thought Mrs Hair must have reprimanded him severely. I thanked God for her. My life returned to normal for many weeks. I thought my ordeal was over. But sadly, it was not.' She stopped to adjust a lock of her hair which had appeared from her bonnet.

'It happened again?' Scougall asked tentatively.

'One night I found myself alone in the kitchen. I heard footsteps in the corridor outside. Then he appeared. I could tell he'd been drinking again. He leapt towards me and tried to fondle me. He started saying vile things. I screamed as loudly as I could. I think he believed everyone had gone home for the night. He smiled lasciviously at me and began to pull up my dress. But, thank God, Mr Galbraith appeared at the door. He had heard me screaming. MacLeod was forced to stop his debauch. As he left the kitchen, he whispered in my ear that if I went to Mrs Hair again to tell her what had happened, he would have me done away with. He would kill me. He would have me drowned in the Nor Loch or pay a friend to have me dealt with. No-one would hear anything of me ever again. I was terrified out of my mind. I didn't know what to do.'

Scougall was reflecting that his initial feelings about MacLeod had been correct. He was a rogue of the first order. 'What did you do, Betty?'

'I hatched a plan to flee the city with the little money I had and make for London. I thought of talking to Mrs Hair again. But I feared if I did so, he would carry out his threat. Again, I spent a sleepless night in despair, thinking I would not go into the office the next morning. I awoke in a fever. I sent a note to Mrs Hair that I was ill. She sent a doctor to see me. I was not able to return to the office for ten days. I did not want to go back but I did not want to disappoint Mrs Hair. Finally, I forced myself to return.'

'What did he do when you went back?'

'There was no sign of him in the office, Mr Scougall. He had not been there for a few days, I was told. He did not appear the next day. I was so relieved. And then another day and another day. I rejoiced in my heart. I prayed to God he was gone for good, perhaps abroad or to the Highlands, as some in the office said. I even prayed some mischief was done to him, God forgive me. I wondered if Mrs Hair had decided to get rid of him. I said nothing to her about it. The days passed. I heard nothing. I heard they had searched his apartments and over the town. Then there was news a body was found. When I read the lines in the *Gazette*, I'm sorry to confess, God forgive me, I hoped it was his body discovered at Craigleith. When I heard it was him, I rejoiced he was no more.' She paused for a moment. Her tone was gentler when she said: 'There you have it, Mr Scougall. That is the fine gentleman folk in the city mourn. The Highland gentleman who is foster-son of a great chief. He was nothing but a common brute. I will not mourn his passing, although the man who killed him is a sinner in the eyes of God, just like the man he killed.'

Scougall was moved by her account which he considered was entirely believable. But he knew he had to remain sceptical.

MacKenzie would question him about whether she was telling the truth. It was possible she could have killed MacLeod or paid someone to do it. She certainly had a strong enough motive. He wondered what question to ask next. He knew MacKenzie would have put her on the spot. But there was an uncomfortable silence as he tried to think of something to ask. He did not want to upset her any further. Suddenly a figure appeared at the door behind them, providing the opportunity for her to excuse herself with a slight curtsy. She removed her apron and left the kitchen before he thought of anything else to say. A thin youth of about fourteen wearing a white shirt and black breeches with shoulder-length hair deposited a pile of dishes on the work bench in the kitchen. He had a friendly open face.

'Good afternoon, sir. I'm Billy Farquharson, apprentice to Mrs Hair.'

Scougall recognised the name. 'You were working with Aeneas MacLeod?'

'That's right, sir. I'm an apprentice. I started here five months ago.'

Scougall smiled warmly, relieved that the interview with Betty was over. He found it much easier to speak to the youth. 'We share the same profession, Mr Farquharson. I'm a notary too. I remember fondly my years as an apprentice with Hugh Dallas. You may have come across his work on conveyancing in your studies.'

'I've a copy of his mighty tome. It is surely our Bible. You know, Mr Scougall, being a notary is much harder work than I thought it would be. After spending a day copying a document I'm exhausted. It requires much concentration and Mr MacLeod was difficult sometimes. He was furious if I made the slightest mistake.'

Scougall was delighted that the boy was answering his questions before he had asked them. 'Were you articled to him?'

'No. He was overseeing my work for a period.'

'How did you find him as a mentor?'

'At first, he was fine enough, but he began to treat me… badly, you know, bully me. Picking over all my work. He would find mistakes everywhere. He would laugh at them and criticise me. Then the next minute it was completely different. He was my best friend. He was taking me out for drinks in a tavern, all paid by him. Then he was angry again when I came into the office late the next morning with a hangover. I would say, I didn't take to him. Although I'm sorry he's dead. No one deserves such an end.'

Scougall reflected that MacLeod made enemies of everyone. 'Why do you think he was killed, Mr Farquharson?'

'I don't know, sir. I've heard lots of stories about him in the office. He was always talked about when he wasn't there.'

'What kind of stories?'

Farquharson paused for a moment, as if he was wondering if he should continue to be so open about MacLeod, but then continued: 'It was said he was a Jacobite, devoted to the cause of the old King. That he had business interests of his own, outside the office. That he lent money on his own book. Also, that he was involved in illicit trading and on good terms with criminals in the city. He provided them with money. I don't know if these stories are true. If you ask me, he seemed to be the kind of man who made enemies.'

Scougall nodded. 'Can you think of anyone who might have wanted to kill him?'

Farquharson looked like he was enjoying himself. Was he relishing the opportunity to get back at a cruel mentor? He moved closer to Scougall and his voice dropped to a whisper. 'I would not, sir. I was not keen on him, I've said that, but I would not do such a thing…'

'I was not suggesting it was you, Billy. But can you think of anyone else?'

The boy thought for a few moments. 'I don't like speaking ill of my colleagues, but Mr Galbraith bore a particular hatred towards him.'

'Why was that?' Scougall wondered why Mrs Hair had not mentioned any antipathy between Galbraith and MacLeod. Perhaps she did not know about it.

'I don't know, exactly, sir. I've heard it was about what MacLeod said about his wife and the identity of the father of her child. MacLeod joked that Galbraith was not the father... that he was not a true man... that he was... I think the word is impotent. When Galbraith overheard him, he was very angry. I've never seen him like that before or since. You could tell he was trying to control himself. I could see him shaking and flexing his fists. Thereafter, I believe he bore a grudge against him. He was always saying: one day, MacLeod will have his come-uppance.'

Scougall was pleased to have discovered something new to give MacKenzie. 'What about the fight between MacLeod and Adam Scobie?'

'It all happened before I came to the office. I've heard about it though. I do not know Scobie myself. He was another who hated MacLeod. I think MacLeod mocked his religion.'

'What about Betty McGrain?'

The boy looked blank. 'What do you mean, sir?'

'It's nothing, Billy.' Scougall realised he might not know anything about what happened between them. 'If you think of anything else please let me know. It's time I was on my way. Perhaps you can show me out?'

CHAPTER 12

MacLeod's Chambers

WHILE SCOUGALL WAS busy in Mrs Hair's office MacKenzie made for Lorimer's Close in the Lawnmarket. Johnstone's Land, where MacLeod had rented chambers, was a large, seven-storey tenement in the courtyard at the bottom of the close. MacKenzie found MacLeod's landlord John Aitken, an old man with long whiskers and a hunched back who invited him into his snug, a small room which acted as an office, sitting room and kitchen. They were soon both puffing away on their pipes in front of a fire which was lit to keep the old man warm although it was a summer's day.

'How did you find MacLeod as a tenant, Mr Aitken?' asked MacKenzie, removing his jacket because it was so warm in the room.

'I found him a good one, Mr MacKenzie. He always paid rent on time. He had done so for many years. He was my tenant for five years or more.'

'Was there ever any trouble with him?'

'Very little compared to the other young men who have taken chambers with me. He was quiet enough, although during his apprentice days, a few years back, there was the usual stuff with drink and whores.' The old man nodded, knowingly.

'Is there anything he might have done or have been involved in that comes to mind in relation to his murder?'

The old man put his index finger on his temple and closed his eyes, still sucking on his pipe. 'One incident springs to mind, sir,' he said. 'On the night of the riot last year, a couple of men came looking for him. I remember it because I was scared about what might happen to my property. The mob was out smashing windows. Anyone suspected of being Papist, or of knowing a Papist, was in danger. We were told to put candles in our windows to support the opposition to the government. I made sure one was lit in every window in every floor to avoid the mob's rage. But MacLeod refused to put one in his window, despite my request. I was annoyed by this. I thought the visit might be related to it. They could be checking whose window it was.'

MacKenzie loosened his necktie. He was beginning to sweat. 'What exactly happened, Mr Aitken?'

'The men kept banging on his door until I was forced to go upstairs to see who it was. I was surprised to find the Captain of the Guard with one of his regulars. They were looking for MacLeod. They had to find him as soon as possible. There was urgency in the request. It made an impression on me. I told them he was away and that he had left in the afternoon to observe events on the street. The Captain said they would be back if they couldn't find him. But I didn't see them at his door again. Fortunately, my window was not smashed. I told MacLeod about their visit the next day. He said it was nothing, just a minor business matter which had been quickly resolved. They had found him. A debt had to be redeemed quickly. I never saw them at his door again. But I remember that occasion well. They looked anxious to find him, as if a life depended on it.'

'You're sure they were Town Guards?' asked MacKenzie, wondering about the possible association between MacLeod and Stein which had also been mentioned by Galbraith. And why was Stein visiting MacLeod on the night of the riot rather than seeing to the security of the city?

'Of course. I've seen them often in uniform. The younger one, the Captain, was a soldier – I think his name is Stein. The other was one of the older ones, I don't know his name, a gangly fellow with an ugly face. I've seen him staggering drunk down the High Street many times.' Aitken pulled a key out of his pocked and handed it to MacKenzie. 'MacLeod's room is on the third floor, Mr MacKenzie.'

'How many copies of this key are there?' he asked.

'Two. This and MacLeod's,' Aitken replied.

'Has anyone else come to look at his chamber?'

'I had a quick look around myself when a boy came from his office asking for him. Everything appeared in order but there was no sign of MacLeod.'

'Did the boy go inside?'

'No. He just asked me if MacLeod was there. I had a quick look and told him there was no sign of him.'

MacKenzie thanked him, rose from his chair and left the snug. He climbed the turnpike stair at the back of the tenement, relieved to be out of the stifling heat. He found the climb a struggle. He recalled scrambling up mountains with his foster brothers as a boy in the Highlands and running along the narrow ridges without a care in the world. Now he was having difficulties with a three-storey climb. He was growing old. It seemed like another world back then. It many ways it was. It was the old world before the civil wars. It was a world written in Gaelic. His foster parents barely spoke a word of English. He looked back on it with a piercing nostalgia. Once he had reached the third floor and located MacLeod's room, he paused for a few moments to gather his breath, then inserted the key into the lock and opened the door slowly. It was immediately obvious that MacLeod's chambers had been ransacked. Furniture was overturned, glasses smashed, pictures knocked off walls, clothing thrown about. He closed the door behind him. This must have occurred after Aitken had come in to look for MacLeod. He looked at the lock on the door. It showed no signs of being forced. He stepped around the debris on the floor and examined the windows in the main room. None were open or broken. They were three storeys up so the chances of someone entering or leaving through one of the windows would have been unlikely. The window was also locked in the bedchamber. He concluded that the rooms must have been turned over after MacLeod's death and a key had been used to enter, probably MacLeod's.

He made a close examination of the apartment. A writing desk was overturned and smashed up in the living chamber. The hearth stood cold with the remnants of coal and ashes lying in the grate. He checked to see if any documents or papers had been burnt in the fire but there was no sign of any. He moved gingerly over the debris on the floor. He checked the pieces of clothing, the books strewn everywhere, old copies of the *Gazette*. In the bedchamber there was a bed, press, table, some wine glasses and rotting food on a plate. A few jackets and some breeches had been thrown onto the floor next to a spilled chamber pot. There was a reek of stale urine. He took out a notebook and made a few jottings. It was clear that most of the activity had been focused around the desk in the living chamber. It was pulverised and it looked like its contents had been taken. No private papers, documents or letters were left in or around the smashed drawers.

After spending half an hour in MacLeod's chambers, he returned the key to the landlord and met Scougall in the Periwig, where they shared a bottle of claret and some oysters.

'Tell me what you've found out, Davie.'

'There was little of interest in MacLeod's office,' began Scougall, hesitantly. 'There was nothing in his desk except the instrument book and, in the other desk, only a copy of the *Gazette*. I went carefully through the instruments in the book. MacLeod was obviously working on a series of property acquisitions for Mrs Hair. I've noted them down here.' He handed a piece of paper to MacKenzie who read the following:

> The sale of Barber's Land by Robert Sinclair to James Brown for 100 pounds.
>
> The sale of a tenement in Byres's Close by Alexander Cockburn to John Butler for 50 pounds.
>
> The sale of Mason's Land in Libberton's Wynd by Patrick Young to Richard Cairns for 75 pounds.

Scougall then described his interviews with Betty McGrain and Billy Farquharson while MacKenzie listened with interest.

Once Scougall had recalled everything, MacKenzie sat back in his seat and lit a pipe.

'I'm impressed, Davie,' he said. 'You've been busy. Now, let me tell you about my visit to MacLeod's rooms. The door was not damaged, nor were the windows, but the interior had been ransacked; MacLeod's desk destroyed. The intruder entered using a key which he or she obtained, no doubt, from MacLeod's pocket. The intruder, who we might postulate was MacLeod's killer, was looking for something in the desk. All MacLeod's papers were taken. The landlord told me he was visited by Captain Stein and his man on the night of the riot.'

They sat in silence for a few minutes. MacKenzie puffed on his pipe, pondering what they had learned, and drinking the wine. Scougall, observing MacKenzie, reflected that he was smoking much more since Elizabeth's disappearance. He must have a word with him when the case was finished, encourage him to smoke less. It was a vile habit!

MacKenzie ordered another bottle of wine and sat back. 'We're making some progress at least, Davie. We have suspects to focus our attention on: Betty McGrain, Galbraith, Scobie and Stein. Perhaps even the boy Farquharson, although I think it's doubtful a youth could have killed MacLeod and transported his body to Craigleith or arranged someone to do it. However, we must keep him in mind.'

'What about Mrs Hair?' Scougall was pleased to be complemented and was enjoying the effects of the wine.

'Of course, Davie. We must not exclude her. Let us consider motives. Betty McGrain might have wanted revenge for her assault. Scobie was insulted by the engravings and challenged him to a duel. Galbraith was upset by remarks about his wife. But was that enough to drive him to commit murder? And let us not forget Mrs Hair?'

'Do you think he did something to upset her, sir?'

'I do not know. And then there's the boy, Farquharson. He's also a possibility, but then, realistically, how many apprentices kill their master for a little bullying?' MacKenzie shook his head. 'I think Stein is definitely connected to MacLeod in some way but we do need to learn more about them all. I propose we first visit the spot where his body was found.'

The next morning, they hired horses in the Cowgate and left the city by the West Port, crossing the Water of Leith at the Dean. It was a pleasant journey in the warm sunshine of a summer afternoon. MacKenzie rode ahead, deep in thought. An unattractive picture was emerging of MacLeod. He was ambitious, duplicitous, arrogant, aggressive, shrewd and calculating, and was not liked by anyone outside his clan. MacKenzie knew many Highlanders like him. The harshness of life there turned many into grasping individuals who would do anything to advance their own interests and cared as much for their fellow creatures as though they were slugs in a garden. But Highlanders could also be loyal, generous, hospitable.

Scougall's mind wandered from the case as his horse trotted along the path. Thoughts of a future wife took hold of him – an end to his loneliness and a focus for his desires. He must marry someone soon, he reflected. He wondered what the lass found by his mother would be like. What he desired above all was a change to his life, something different from his routine of legal work and nights alone at Mrs Baird's.

It was a two-mile ride to the quarry at Craigleith, a great hole gouged out of the ground by generations of quarriers which was the main source of honey-coloured sandstone for the city. As they approached the amphitheatre of rock, they could hear the ringing of hammers on the stone. An army of quarriers was busy at work. At the edge of the quarry was an ancient wooden shack. Smoke drifted from a metal chimney. MacKenzie knocked on the ramshackle door and shouted that he was looking for the man who had found MacLeod's body. A disgruntled quarrier appeared. 'I found him, sir. Dod Shanks is my name. What's it to do with you?'

MacKenzie explained the reason for their visit. 'Could you show us where you found the body, Mr Shanks? I have a shilling here, if you'll help us.' The quarrier looked down on the coin avariciously, then went back inside. They could hear muffled conversation before he reappeared, wearing his jacket and hat. 'The master has given me permission. This way, gentlemen.'

They followed Shanks out of the quarry and along a path to the south which wound through the rolling countryside; nature was at its most prolific in the heavy summer. Emerging from a copse of birch, they came into an open piece of land facing a sandstone cliff about twenty feet in height. At the top of the rockface was a clump of birch trees, their roots dangling out of the earth. Beneath them was a mound of stone and earth.

'The storm caused a landslide here,' said Shanks, indicating the cliff.

'What happened on the day after the storm?' asked MacKenzie.

'Everywhere was flooded as far as the eye could see, especially the lower ground,' replied Shanks. 'The whole place was like a huge loch with wee islands sticking up here and there. The quarry was completely under water. We couldn't get in to work the stone until the water had gone down. The master told me to have a wander round to see if any damage had been done to the surrounding land. The landslide drew my attention right away – it was something different from the usual view. I came up to get a closer look and then saw a body lying face down amongst the rubble.'

'Can you show me where exactly you saw him?' asked MacKenzie.

Shanks walked forward a couple of yards and indicated with his stick. 'He lay about here. His head was pointing west.'

'Did you move the body?' asked Scougall.

Shanks shook his head. 'I went straight back to tell the master and then some men came for him with a cart. We lifted him in and he was taken back to Edinburgh.'

'Did anyone see anything suspicious around here before or after the storm?' asked MacKenzie, observing Shanks.

'How do you mean, sir?'

'In the days or weeks before the storm, was anyone seen looking around, as if searching for a place to bury a body?'

'I don't believe so, sir.'

Scougall turned to MacKenzie, 'Why do you think he was brought out here specifically, sir?'

'A convenient place to dispose of a body. A wild piece of land not far from the city.' MacKenzie shrugged. 'MacLeod would still be under the earth if it wasn't for the storm – the killer was unlucky. MacLeod might've lain buried for a thousand years.'

The three men turned and retraced their steps towards the quarry. On the way, something caught MacKenzie's eye. It looked incongruous lying in the grass at the side of the path. He knelt down to see what it was, then picked it up and slipped it into his pocket. It was strange to find it there, so out of place in the grass. Back at the quarry, they had another look around. Scougall noticed a line of carts near the entrance. The horses had been taken away to be fed. 'Do these take the stone to the city, Mr Shanks?' he asked.

'Yes, sir.'

'What happens to the empty ones once the stone is delivered to Edinburgh?' asked MacKenzie.

'They're brought back in the late afternoon or evening by the cart man.'

MacKenzie turned to Scougall. 'There you go, Davie; a convenient way to transport a body out of the city with little suspicion, on the back of a cart, preferably in the dark.'

MacKenzie walked over to the first cart. He rummaged in the back, pulling back filthy tarpaulins, then moved onto the next one and the next. He called Scougall over. 'Look here, Davie, on the floor at the back. They look like bloodstains!' Scougall climbed up to get a close look. There was a large dark stain across the bottom of the cart.

'Who took this cart back to the quarry before the storm?' asked MacKenzie, turning to look back at Shanks.

'Our cart driver, Rab Christie,' answered Shanks, who had joined them at the bloodstained cart.

'I would like to speak with him,' said MacKenzie.

'That won't be possible, sir. He's disappeared into thin air. That was the last job he did. We're looking for another carter to replace him.'

'Do you know what's happened to him?' MacKenzie said quickly, climbing back out of the cart and looking alarmed.

'No idea. He never turned up for work one day. The master was furious. Fortunately, it's quiet just now because of all the disruptions.'

'When was this, Mr Shanks?'

'He disappeared a couple of days before the storm. No sign of him since.'

'Did he live in the city?'

'I believe so. He rented a chamber in the Cowgate with his young brother in a tenement in Leitch's Close. There's no sign of him there though or his brother. They've both disappeared into thin air.'

CHAPTER 13

A Pint at Gourlay's

BACK IN TOWN, MacKenzie had much to think about. The visit to the quarry had raised more questions about the murder. As he and Scougall walked down the High Street, MacKenzie's thoughts turned to George Gourlay, a well-known figure in the city, especially among lawyers. Gourlay might be a useful source of information about MacLeod. He had owned a tavern just off the Cowgate for years, but had other business interests which included whoremongering, extortion, forging, blackmail and robbery. Gourlay also dealt in certain illicit goods: liquor, tobacco and arms. But for a variety of reasons, the Advocate was never able to make a legal case against him stick and he remained at large, untouched by the law. Witnesses decided not to testify at the last moment or left the city suddenly or disappeared; families of victims were compensated with large sums of money and cases dropped. MacKenzie told Scougall about him as they descended the steep slope of the Bow and entered the Grassmarket under the looming castle rock.

'Gourlay has moved into more lucrative businesses like arms and slaves where the margin of profit is higher. It's said most of the shops and taverns around his howff pay him protection money, although they will deny it. There was a time of killings in the past – a battle for dominance in the city. Archibald knows Gourlay well. He tried to convict him on many occasions when he was Crown Officer, but always failed.' MacKenzie stopped talking for a few moments to let a coach and horses rumble past them. 'Besides, Gourlay has been useful to the government as a source of information. He's provided evidence to convict others, usually his enemies. It's unclear if they were any worse than him. But he does follow a moral code of sorts. He looks after his own and polices his territory with an iron fist, providing a sense of security. The government is happy to let things lie as long as there's not too much trouble.'

'Where does he hail from?' asked Scougall as they turned into the Cowgate at the bottom of the Bow and passed St Magdalene's Chapel on their right where they were forced to make way for a herd of cattle on their way to market.

'I don't know who spawned him or when or where he was raised', continued MacKenzie. 'There's a slight Irish inflection to his voice, so he may be from there. I've heard he was a sailor before settling in Leith and moving up to Edinburgh years ago. It's said he won his tavern in a game of cards. It was the beginning of his wealth. But it's probably just a story. He no doubt purchased it for a song and expanded by buying neighbouring tenements as they came on the market.'

Gourlay's howff was in a part of the city rarely frequented by lawyers like MacKenzie and Scougall. It was in the middle of a densely packed warren of stinking lanes wrapped around ancient and decrepit tenements built in the distant past, some said as far back as the days of Alexander III. The howff itself was a sprawling conglomerate of wood and stone, part house, part tower, reconstructed by war, demolition and fire. An inconspicuous door with peeling green paint in a squalid street at the bottom of a turnpike stair was the main entrance, although it was said there were other secret ways in and out around the city. A person unfamiliar with the place, a newcomer to the city, might have passed the door as insignificant, however, the establishment was famous for serving customers every hour of the day on every day of the week, even the Sabbath, for the Kirk held no sway behind Gourlay's door. Scougall had never walked down the vennel in his life. It had a reputation of danger. The urchins and orphans living there were notorious for stoning anyone in a good suit, particularly writers. MacKenzie judged he had not been inside its smoky interior for a dozen years. Gourlay's was a port for the restless and troubled, a refuge for the mad and insane, poor and desperate, who gravitated towards its dark chambers like moths to a candle flame. It offered escape from the pain of this mortal coil. Behind its door you could forget everything for a few hours. Within its walls, all manner of debauchery and rebellion were dreamt up and anything could be bought, from a slave girl to a parrot, or gambled for cards or dice, as long as payment was in hard cash. It was a small enclave in the city outside the law, a colony of sin within the heart of Edinburgh. Its existence was hated by the righteous. It was remarkable it survived at all, thought MacKenzie. But such places were found in every city he had ever visited. Corruption, perversity and debauchery were among the few certainties in human life.

'Why does the council allow it to flourish?' asked Scougall timidly as they entered the low doorway.

'Gourlay has friends in high places, Davie. Both in church and state, and on the town council. They turn a blind eye to his activities. To bother him might be stirring up a hornet's nest.'

'How do you mean, sir?'

'I've heard it said Gourlay has dirt on every politician who saw the light of day, and on plenty of ministers and elders of the Kirk. Many have visited his tavern over the years to partake in illicit pleasures. He keeps a record of attendance and a list of their particular tastes.'

'Dirt?' Scougall asked, unfamiliar with the word in this context.

'The filth which clings to most men in high places. He's bribed every whore in the city. He has eyes and ears everywhere. It's said he has a book recording the perversities of the unco guid – Gourlay's Good Book is famous! I don't know if it actually exists, but it would make an interesting read. Maybe we can ask him about it, Davie.'

'We've come to meet him?' asked Scougall, his expression not hiding his trepidation. MacKenzie nodded and they entered.

Despite the decrepit walls of the tenement outside, the interior was not as grim as Scougall had expected, nor was it entirely inhabited by the monsters of his imagination, indeed he was surprised to recognise a few faces – lawyers and merchants he knew by sight. The howff was much larger than seemed possible from the outside, extending through a series of low-ceilinged rooms smoky but warm, with numerous hearths and small private snugs and dining rooms sprouting off the main chambers. There were no windows, but a multitude of candles flickered in brackets on the walls and on the low tables. A man in a plaid scratched a fiddle in one corner. A plethora of dogs of every conceivable breed languished on the stone, straw-covered floor.

Because of the early hour, the establishment was not busy, but it was still doing a reasonable trade – a few drunks sprawled in corners or were slumped over one of the many wooden tables. Bar maids carrying trays circulated, while whores wandered provocatively selling their wares and leading customers off to darker chambers among the labyrinth of rooms down a set of dimly-lit stairs.

MacKenzie found an empty snug offering a good view of the main hall. They sank into a leather settee like stones in quicksand. Scougall had the feeling that once ensconced it would be difficult to get up again after a few drinks.

Within a couple of minutes, a maid approached them. MacKenzie ordered a bottle of claret and some mince pies. The wine and food was swiftly delivered and Scougall comforted himself with a large glass to curtail his nervousness.

As he paid the barmaid, MacKenzie asked her: 'Tell Gourlay the old Clerk of Session would like a word with him, if he has time.' She nodded. 'Is there anything else I can get you, gentlemen? The company of a couple of lassies?' Scougall was shocked by the suggestion. 'That's all just now', added MacKenzie, smiling warmly, sensing with amusement Scougall's discomfort.

The pies were delicious and the wine began to calm Scougall's nerves, allowing him to observe his surroundings in more detail. It really wasn't as bad as he had feared. He had expected to see brawling sailors and angry drunks everywhere.

At length, he spotted a large, bald man limping towards them, aided by a stick. The man bowed his head to enter the snug.

'It's been too long, MacKenzie,' he said, giving MacKenzie his hand. 'Who's this rogue you drink with?'

'My assistant, Davie Scougall. A notary with a steady hand,' MacKenzie returned the handshake smiling, and Gourlay turned to Scougall.

'I'm pleased to meet you, sir. I like a man with a steady hand. I'm always pleased to see men of law enjoying their leisure in my establishment.' Scougall nodded nervously. He was transfixed by Gourlay's unusual appearance. He had seen nothing like him before in his life. The stark baldness of his head reminded him of the giant egg of some monstrous bird. His arms and neck were covered in tattoos of strange animals. His grin was entirely toothless.

'Will you take a glass with us, George?' asked MacKenzie.

Gourlay dropped himself into the seat opposite them and MacKenzie filled another glass. Scougall could smell a pungent mixture of rum and sweat. He was close enough to see there were numerous scars among the tattoos. He found himself mesmerised by images of ships, mermaids, whales and dolphins.

'The creatures of the deep are a marvel are they not, Mr Scougall,' laughed Gourlay, noticing Scougall's interest. 'They remind me of my years at sea as a boy and young man. If we had time, I might've entertained you with a tale or two of the Caribbean or of the vast pirate island of Madagascar, but sadly I'm busy with business. What can I do for you, gentlemen?'

MacKenzie decided to waste no more time on small talk. 'I'm investigating a killing.'

Gourlay's face opened into a broad smile. He looked like a dog that had just been presented with a bone or heard his master at the gate. 'A killing is it? Not another killing in this city. Another killing. So many killings. Which one do you refer to, MacKenzie?'

'A young lawyer called Aeneas MacLeod. His body was found after the storm at Craigleith Quarry; his throat cut. A landslide caused by the storm opened his grave.'

Gourlay nodded thoughtfully. 'I've heard about it. He's the one who worked for Mrs Hair?'

'The MacLeods have asked me to investigate his death. They want to know who killed him and why. The Advocate has little time for the case himself. He's bogged down in... politics.'

'We miss the old Crown Officer, indeed, do we not, Mr MacKenzie. Your friend, Stirling. All of us miss him very much. He was often a customer in my establishment. I was always able to look after his...' Gourlay changed tack, '...to serve his needs. I've not seen him for some time. Is he well?'

'His time is taken up with arranging the marriage of his daughter,' replied MacKenzie.

'I could've married one of my sons to her. We might have forged a bond between our families... I've heard MacLeod was a bit of a rogue.'

'What do you mean?' asked MacKenzie, his interest piqued.

Gourlay lowered his voice, 'I've heard he was up to tricks. He was getting deep in dirty business.'

'What kind of dirty business?' MacKenzie asked, leaning in towards Gourlay, keen to hear more.

'The business of extorting money from the good folk of Edinburgh. Taking the lessons of blackmail, no doubt learned in the Highlands as a bairn, and applying them in this city.'

'Blackmail?'

'Aye. An evil business!'

'Who was he trying to blackmail?' asked MacKenzie.

'He was trying to make a name for himself. Trying to establish himself as a bit of a rough man about town... a man folk feared. He's obviously upset someone... stepped on someone's toes. I've heard it's a risky business!'

MacKenzie dropped his voice to a whisper and moved his head towards Gourlay. His expression darkened and there was no hint of humour when he asked: 'Did he upset you, George?'

Gourlay looked down at his large butcher's hands. 'I've no time to trouble myself with a minnow like MacLeod. He was a tiny fish in this pool. He dared not infringe on me. But there are other fish in the drumly waters. Behold, a new pike is swimming against me, I might say. I might call him that because I'll soon have to deal with him.'

'Who is the pike?' asked MacKenzie.

Gourlay finished his drink and belched, before wiping his mouth on his stained, shirt sleeve. 'You might have heard of him. He's called Stein, Captain of the Guard. He was a soldier for the old King. He now tries to cause a stir here. He's a newcomer but already has a finger in too many pies. He's trying to raise protection money from parts of the city which he has no right to. His approach is too reckless for my liking. He does not follow the rules of the game. He's too quick in the way he does business. He threatens clients too readily. He does not build up relations, establish trust. He does not... how will I put it... he's too brutal in his methods.'

'Too brutal for George Gourlay?' MacKenzie sat back and smiled.

'I would never say that,' Gourlay replied, shaking his head ruefully.

'Are you telling us MacLeod was connected to Stein in some way?'

Gourlay hesitated for a moment. He moved his stick from one hand to the other and turned it to face them. The head of a snarling dog was carved on the tip. 'I believe they were known to each other.'

'In what way?'

'I've heard they were partners. I know not the exact details of their relations. But they both fancied themselves as men who could make up the rules. Perhaps MacLeod was the brains and Stein the brawn.'

'Do you know anything more about his killing, George?'

Gourlay smiled and shook his head slowly. 'A dreadful business. I've heard MacLeod called... well, I've heard him called a Jacobite... but that's hardly anything to be called these days. I've heard it said he had a liking for young maidens, but is that a sin, gentlemen? If I learn anything more, about his killer or killers, I'll let you know.' Gourlay began to rise painfully from the table using his stick but MacKenzie continued to question him.

'Who wanted him dead?' asked MacKenzie.

Gourlay raised his great head again and stared intently at MacKenzie. 'I don't know, Mr MacKenzie. I can assure you of one thing. It was not me.'

'Was it the government or the Presbyterians? Or was it Stein?' MacKenzie pressed on.

Gourlay smiled. 'Or all three of them? These are difficult days for our country, for the whole of Britain. It's a time of flux. There will be winners and losers. MacLeod was one of the losers. Others will rise in his place.'

MacKenzie shook his head. 'A time of flux, indeed. A bloody flux. We'll not keep you much longer. Just one final question. On another matter. What do you know about the explosion in the Canongate?'

'A nasty business!' Gourlay exclaimed and then stopped, looking suspicious. 'You're surely not suggesting I was behind it? It's not my style, gentlemen. So much noise in public. Such a stir! They heard it all the way to Lithgow! I like to keep things a little less conspicuous. It's the best way to do business.'

'Stein's man was killed in the explosion. Stein himself was injured.'

Gourlay raised his eyebrows. 'I've heard that was the case. My son read me the details in the *Gazette*. Was Stein the target of the powder? I do not know. It's claimed Jacobites were responsible or it was a terrible accident. Storing powder under your house is stupid. Why was it not kept in a storeroom in Leith? Some hot head is no doubt behind it.'

'Do you take a political position, Mr Gourlay?' Scougall suddenly asked, finally summoning up the courage to ask a question. He had sat silently until then with a hundred questions forming in his mind but he found himself tongue-tied as usual.

'The notary has a tongue after all!' laughed Gourlay. 'I would not be so stupid, Mr Scougall. I've no interest in politics. I'm only interested in politicians. I'm interested in the men who follow the trade of politics. Their actual position does not concern me, unless it affects my trade, unless it increases the price of my wine or beer, unless they plant impositions on my goods. That is my politics. I've had to fight through life, gentlemen. No one ever did George Gourlay any favours in this world. My mother and father were dead before I was three. I've had a hard life. Man is not made in the image of God as the kirkmen tell us. That's what I learned at a young age. I saw a man killed in front of me when I was an eight-year-old bairn. His neck slashed, his blood gushing all over me. I saw torture, beyond your imagination, at sea. Pirates flayed their captives alive and threw bairns to the sharks. I had to learn quickly to survive. Everything I have built up here is down to my own hard work. There was no parish school for George Gourlay. There was no university education. The sea was my education. I learned everything I know onboard ship. Of this powder plot, I know nothing. But I'll tell you if I learn anything more about MacLeod. You're not a bad one for a lawyer, MacKenzie.' He clapped MacKenzie on the shoulder and made to turn away, 'Now I must leave you to your victuals, gentlemen.'

CHAPTER 14

Captain of the Guard

WHEN MACKENZIE AND SCOUGALL emerged from Gourlay's it was already growing dark. They walked back up to the High Street in the gloaming towards the Tollbooth. MacKenzie opened the low door and, without hesitation, headed left for the Guard Room. He knew the place well. Without knocking, they entered a low-ceilinged chamber with a roaring fire. Three men lounged on chairs before it, warming their feet. The room smelt stale and felt oppressive.

'Good evening, gentlemen,' said MacKenzie, raising his voice and catching the guards by surprise. They fumbled to their feet, then recognising him, slumped back.

'Oh, Mr MacKenzie, it's you, sir. It's been too long, and Mr Scougall as well,' said one of the guards, a thin, grey-haired man, nodding his head at the newcomers.

'We're looking for a word with Captain Stein, Mr Campbell,' said MacKenzie, casually.

'Stein is through there,' said Campbell, pointing at a closed door and yawning at the same time. He moved gingerly in his socks across the stone floor. Knocking on the interior door, he peeped in, mumbled something and closed it again. 'He'll be with you in a minute. He's just finishing some business.' MacKenzie nodded his thanks and moved further into the room, Scougall at his shoulder.

'How are you, Mr Campbell?' he asked.

'I'm well, sir. I was sorry to hear about your trouble, with your daughter, and your fall with Mr Stirling – such changes in the kingdom in the last year. Who would've predicted it? Mr Stirling was popular here, sir. Always generous with the men. He knew how to hand out drink money. Not like the new crew who rule us now! A cold dish of kail is the grim creature who is Advocate and no Crown Officer appointed yet. Not generous like Stirling, sir. Not like the auld days. Only obsessed with one thing – obtaining value for money. Dents the moral of the men, if they don't get drink money. They'd hoped to benefit from the Revolution with a pay rise. See a bit more siller coming their way after all the hard work they do for the city. We hoped it would increase the generosity of the government towards us. As you know, we're vital for folk's safety. But we were quickly forgotten in the turmoil of the times. We're still the laughing stock of many. We're even abused by urchins on the street. But Captain Stein improves things. I believe he will... he's a committed man. Yes, a committed man.'

'You did little to preserve our safety during the riot last December.' Scougall could not help blurting out angrily, remembering how the guard did nothing to stop the killing spree on the streets that he had witnessed himself. He had little respect for the guard who he regarded as self-serving drunken louts, a common view among the citizens of Edinburgh.

'We did what we could, Mr Scougall,' said Campbell, put out by his criticism. 'There were thousands on the street that night. We were only a few brave men. Twenty guards to look after a city and we're never paid on time. What could we do against a rabble of thousands!'

'How is your new captain?' asked MacKenzie quickly, seeking to change the conversation before Scougall could reply.

Campbell hesitated for a moment. 'I believe respect for us will rise under Captain Stein. But it's early days, gentlemen. He has great plans for us. Changes are afoot and the men grumble about it. Too much change unnerves us. But I believe he will do us some good.'

Before he could elaborate, the inner door opened. A man in the garb of a merchant emerged and left quickly without greeting anyone. Another figure appeared at the door. Scougall assumed it was Stein and was surprised to see that he was younger than the other guards; a powerfully built man, smartly dressed in frock coat and silk cravat with an impressive wig on his head. He smiled and shook hands with them warmly. 'Welcome, Mr MacKenzie, Mr Scougall. Please come into the office, as I call it.'

They followed him into a small, windowless chamber. MacKenzie knew it was situated at the heart of the Tollbooth. A couple of candles provided the only light. The furniture in the room was sparse: an old desk and a few chairs, while along the walls, lay piles of weapons, mostly swords, muskets and pistols. Scougall glanced at the latter objects. Noticing his look, Stein said, 'You look nervous, Mr Scougall? I'm a soldier by trade. I take particular interest in the weaponry of war. They are my tools just as pen and ink are yours. You're lucky to make a living with the tools of peace.' Stein indicated they were to sit in the two chairs facing the desk. 'It's interesting how weapons are changed and improved over the years. I've ideas myself how to improve the musket, how to make it more accurate and fire a greater distance. Those new ones there are from Holland. They will replace older pieces which are unreliable and dangerous for the men to use. My plan is to improve the Guard by arming them properly and training them, but getting money from the government is a struggle, especially with the Jacobite rebellion in the north. All available money is diverted to MacKay's army. At least that's what Dalrymple tells me. It's difficult to maintain morale among the men if they are not paid.' He then indicated a bottle on his desk. 'You'll join me in a glass, gentlemen?' He filled three glasses from a pewter wine jug. 'Good health! What brings you to the Tollbooth on this summer's evening?'

MacKenzie began affably. 'It's a business matter, Captain Stein. I'm acting for a client in a criminal case. You may have heard about it. I'm acting for the kin of Aeneas MacLeod, a writer found at Craigleith Quarry with his throat cut.' MacKenzie waited to observe Stein's response, but there was no indication of any change to his expression.

Stein emptied his glass and filled another. 'It may be the killing was a lawful one, Mr MacKenzie,' he said sardonically.

'What do you mean?'

'I've heard it said more than once on the street that MacLeod was a Jacobite. He was plotting against the government. He met a fitting end for plotting against the King. The punishment for treason is death.'

'He was not tried, Mr Stein. His throat was cut by a person unknown. He was dumped in a dark pit before going before judge and jury.'

'All I'm saying is that during a time of insecurity we cannot be too precious. That's what the government say if I ask them. If we are to preserve the gains of the Revolution, the establishment of a Protestant King and Queen, we must seek out and crush all dissent. If we wish to extend the Revolution further by bringing back a Presbyterian settlement to the Kirk, we must destroy those who seek the return of a Papist King. That's what my masters keep telling me. It's not my own view, Mr MacKenzie. I take no strong view on religion, although I broadly support the Revolution. I focus on practical matters. I attend my men. I'm not a politician, gentlemen, just a simple soldier. And my view is a simple one: kill before you are killed. That was my view on the battlefield and it's my view now in Edinburgh. It's a time of war in the land. Other rules apply when a rebel army wanders the kingdom. A rebel army which has supporters in the taverns and tenements of this city. Dundee's army seeks to smash the Whigs, destroy them and crush them to nothing. The Jacobites will slaughter every last man if they can. If there is evidence of plotting which seems reasonable to the government, surely they are justified in acting. Perhaps I make my politics too transparent for you. I've no sympathy for the old King, although I fought alongside Dundee on the Continent. He's a brave enough man, but a misguided one beholden to a Papist fool. The Stuart dragged us into wars and spent all our money. King William will protect the rights of Protestants. His rule will be beneficial for trade. A close link with the Dutch will help this country. It will allow us to create wealth and better ourselves. The Stuart have held Scotland back for too long!'

Scougall had to admit he agreed with Stein. He almost said 'Aye, indeed' under his breath, but managed to restrain himself, not wanting to annoy MacKenzie.

'Are you involved in trade too, Mr Stein?' asked MacKenzie. 'I thought you just a dull soldier.'

Stein smiled. 'You are partly right, Mr MacKenzie. I'm first and foremost Captain of the Town Guard. That is my *raison d'etre*, as they say. However, I do dabble a little in trade. I buy and sell arms for my men. I know the true value of the instruments of war. I know when a weapon is too expensive and when it's cheap. All my transactions do this city and nation some good. All my actions benefit the Guard. My trade makes the city of Edinburgh safer.'

'And you richer,' added MacKenzie.

'I earn a little from it, but I'm paid next to nothing for my work here!'

'Have you heard anything among the men about the killing or anything on the street?' asked MacKenzie, bringing the conversation back to the matter at hand.

Stein filled their glasses again. 'Only what is written in news sheets and pamphlets. He was found at Craigleith with his throat cut. As I said, he's believed to have links with Jacobites. I know Dalrymple was watching him closely. He had spies following him. I know that because he told me himself. MacLeod was on a list of Jacobite suspects in the city. He was not the kind of man I would have anything to do with.'

'None of the guards have heard anything more?'

'I've heard he was a canny lawyer. I've heard he was aiming high, as we all are, but deep in politics. It's dangerous to be too favourable to the old King in Edinburgh today. The Society folk have assassins who will kill Jacobites without a second thought. The government want to destroy the network here in case Dundee is victorious in the north. There is sense in this strategy from a military point of view. If Dundee is victorious, the Jacobites will become more confident. I will be one of the first they target. If you ask me, look for your assassin of MacLeod among the Covenanters.'

Scougall, listening to Stein's words, wondered if Scobie could be the killer. His family were Covenanting folk after all, and he had a motive.

'You appear,' continued MacKenzie, 'How can I put this... an articulate man to be employed in the Guard?'

'You flatter me, Mr MacKenzie. I've suffered bad fortune in life. I was forced out of my regiment, wrongly accused of corruption, looked down on as a humble man by those who call themselves officers, those who could buy commissions because they were the sons of the nobility or belonged to families with money. But they were the first to shit themselves when they heard a gun fired in battle. I was wrongly accused of irregularities in requisitioning by a man who wanted me out of the way because I was a better soldier than him. And so, I was forced to take this position to make a living until my other interests grow. But I'll use it to my benefit, why shouldn't I? I'll not be Captain of the Town Guard for ever. I aim to become a man of business in this city, that's my ambition, to become a merchant of this good town. Who knows, I may even buy a tavern and call it Andrew Stein's. One day I'll be elected burgess and sit on the council. One day I may be Lord Provost and all those who despised me as a piece of shit for being a bastard will have to swallow their words!' He gave MacKenzie a defiant look, as if daring him to say otherwise. But instead MacKenzie quietly asked, 'like George Gourlay?' Stein hesitated for a moment, MacKenzie noting a hint of anger on his face now. There was a slight twitching of the muscle on the side of his cheek. Perhaps it was the wine that was having an effect, loosening his self-control. 'Gourlay. Aye. Gourlay has done well for a piece of Irish shite!'

'Mr Gourlay says you are precocious in your business interests. He believes you are standing on toes, his toes in particular!'

'I trade in swords and muskets, using contacts from my days as a soldier, Mr MacKenzie. He's not pleased I've entered this business. He wants to control all the arms coming into Edinburgh, so he can fix their price. He does not like honest competition. I provide better value for my clients. I make less profit than he does. He does not like that I push the price down.'

'What about the other lines of business Gourlay is involved in?'

'What do you mean, sir?'

MacKenzie's mask of affability dropped suddenly like the blade of an axe. He spoke harshly to Stein, glowering at him darkly: 'Blackmail, extortion, protection, whoremongering, usury, to name a few.'

Stein observed MacKenzie carefully. He looked unperturbed. He had regained control. He refilled their glasses and MacKenzie saw that his good humour had returned.

'Mr Gourlay may have such interests. I don't have time to keep a brood of whores. I'm an honest man of business. How can I put this, I'm not afraid to fight if I must. I'm ambitious to be a merchant and you must stand up for yourself in this city. How else can you survive? And besides, Gourlay is getting old. His sons are not cut from the same block. They have been educated at school. One has been sent to university to study the law. They have been spoilt by the wealth accumulated by him and so they are weak. He fears everything he has built up will fade as he grows older. Others will rise in his place. It is surely the natural way of things.'

MacKenzie was silent for a few moments, digesting what he had learned. He took his pipe out, packed it with tobacco and lit it.

'Gourlay will fight back hard.' MacKenzie's demeanour lightened as he began to suck on his pipe. 'Your life might be in danger. Your man was killed in the Canongate explosion and you were hurt.'

'He was not my man. He was a member of the Guard. Yes, I'm lucky to be alive. I was in the house five minutes before the explosion. I'd just come out onto the street.'

MacKenzie was surprised by this revelation. He stole a look at Scougall who was scribbling in his notebook. 'I didn't realise you were inside the house,' said MacKenzie. 'It was not mentioned in Jabb's *Gazette*.'

'Like all newsmongers, Jabb does not know the whole picture. Or he keeps details back to reveal them later, so he can make as much as he can from misfortune. An attempt on the life of the Captain of the Guard frightens people and will sell more copies.'

'You know him?'

'He's known to the Guards. I've shared a bottle with him. It's good to know what's going on. Above all, Jabb wants information. He wants stories; he wants dirt and scandal, the misdemeanours of ministers, lawyers and merchants, those who set themselves up as moral guardians of this city. Stories of noblemen's daughters in the company of rakes. Some guards give him real tales and some lie for money.'

'Some say Jabb is a spy, Captain Stein.'

'I would not be surprised if he was, Mr MacKenzie. A man must take money where he can in this world.' Stein laughed and filled his glass again. 'Governments pay handsomely when they are trying to save their own skin. Jabb is interested in one thing, like most men. He seeks to accumulate cash and he's found a novel way of doing it. Feeding news to the people, selling tales of who beds who. It's an ingenious road to riches. But he needs stories with a grain of truth in them. If he makes it all up and is found out, who will buy his paper then?'

'One final question, Captain Stein. Do you supply weapons to the armies in the Highlands?'

'I supply MacKay, not Dundee. I'm a small trader with insufficient capital to compete with merchants like Dunlop, Slight and Gourlay. I cannot buy ordnance. With more funds, I would source artillery pieces in the Low Countries.'

'Dunlop and Slight are dead,' added Scougall, raising his head from his notebook.

Stein nodded. 'Others will enter the market soon. It will not just be me and Gourlay.'

'And if Dundee is successful?' asked MacKenzie.

'I do not believe he will be. I would bet good money on it. A Highland Army, in my judgement, is good for only a short while. The men quickly lose interest in fighting and run off home! Dundee is an old acquaintance. If he's victorious by some miracle, I'll welcome him at the gates of the city and sell him muskets. I'll sell them to King James. But it will not come to that. William is too clever to be defeated by Dundee. The rich merchants of England and Holland support him, while James relies on Louis, a mad Papist King who has bankrupt France. Money will win the war. War is the father of all things, but money is the sinews of war or is it the father of war too? Dundee will be crushed eventually and then...' Stein waited for a few moments before continuing, 'all the Jacobites in this city will be culled.' He tried to fill his glass again but the bottle was empty. 'Perhaps MacLeod was the first to be dispatched. Then there will be no more toasting the king over the water! I do not pick sides, gentlemen. But I would be very careful, if I were you. I would be very careful about showing any support for the Old King.'

CHAPTER 15

A Ride to Ravelston

AFTER BREAKFAST IN MACKENZIE'S chambers they hired horses in the Cowgate and rode out to the small township of Ravelston, a mile south west of Edinburgh, where MacKenzie had learned Dod Shanks lived with his family. MacKenzie wanted to question him again. Scougall was reluctant to go on the Sabbath as he did not like to miss church but MacKenzie was adamant. In half an hour they had reached the tiny hamlet of half a dozen squat dwellings outside the gates of Ravelston House. A couple of men were talking at the door of a cottage. Scougall recognised Shanks was one of them.

MacKenzie dismounted his horse and Scougall got down inelegantly. Shanks looked worried by their arrival. 'Good morning, Mr Shanks. Sorry to disturb your morning smoke. We've a few more questions for you. Can we talk somewhere?' asked MacKenzie, bluntly. Shanks's companion, a younger man, disappeared inside the cottage. Shanks reluctantly led them to a small stone bridge which arched over a meandering stream about fifty yards from the settlement.

'I've told you everything, sir,' he said, stonily. He was clearly annoyed to be disturbed at home.

'Have you, indeed, Mr Shanks. I do not believe you.'

'I swear I have, sir.'

'Did you take anything from MacLeod's body?' MacKenzie's voice was almost threatening. Scougall felt awkward by the turn of questioning and was not sure why MacKenzie had taken such an aggressive approach.

'No, sir. I swear it.' Shanks looked down at his boots, nervously.

MacKenzie put his hand forward and opened his fist to reveal a pencil stub. 'Did you find this?' Dodds stared down at it. He was evidently trying to think of something to say. 'Did you throw this away as you left MacLeod's body?' MacKenzie persisted. Shanks did not answer. There was panic on his face. 'I found a secret pocket in MacLeod's coat,' continued MacKenzie. 'It was empty. Did you find anything in it?' When Shanks continued not to speak, MacKenzie said angrily, 'If you don't tell me the truth, man, I'll march up the drive to Ravelston House this minute and tell Sir John, who's a friend of mine, that you pilfered a dead body!'

Shanks's face turned pale. 'Please, sir. I'm a poor man. I've a wife and bairns to feed.' MacKenzie turned on his heels and headed towards the drive, Scougall following him, a couple of steps behind.

Shanks moved in front of them. 'Stop, sir. Please. I'll tell you everything. I don't want any trouble with the laird. I admit I searched his pockets. But I found very little.'

'You found a pencil stub?' interrupted MacKenzie.

'Yes. I threw it away. It was no use to me. I swear there was no money on him. Just one thing. In the hidden pocket. A sodden lump of paper. I still have it. I'll bring it to you. You can take it away with you. There was no coin on him, I swear it.' Shanks sped off to the hamlet and entered a dwelling.

'I was wondering why this stub was dropped in the middle of nowhere,' explained MacKenzie to Scougall who was looking puzzled. 'Every writer has one in his pocket. It was a reasonable postulation that it belonged to MacLeod.' Scougall reflected that he should be more forceful in his questioning but it just went against his cautious nature.

Shanks emerged a minute later and handed a small dark lump of paper to MacKenzie. 'It has dried out, somewhat. I put it in the ingle. It was sodden when I found it.'

MacKenzie spoke angrily again: 'Is there anything else, man? Tell us the truth this time.'

'I swear, sir. Nothing. Not a penny on him. God forgive me, I shouldn't have taken it. But I just hoped for a few shillings.

He was a lawyer after all. He charged his clients high fees no doubt. Why should he be rich and I poor? Why do I have to dig stone all day in a quarry while he sat in a warm office?'

MacKenzie handed the paper to Scougall. 'Take it, Davie. We'll examine it at the Hawthorns. Let's spend the rest of the Sabbath there.' He turned to Shanks. 'If I find you've been lying to us, Sir John will learn of it.'

'I swear on the lives of my bairns, I found nothing else, sir.'

They mounted their horses, leaving Shanks looking worried.

CHAPTER 16

Reflections of a Jacobite

DEWARTON SAT IN THE SNUG, waiting for them. He was worried about the proliferation of spies in the city, although Gourlay assured him he would deal with any who entered his howff. Spies were everywhere, crawling everywhere, like lice on a mingy dog.

He was worried about the King's cause. MacLeod had held the view of the opposing faction to him, the faction that argued for immediate action, a drastic deed, such as the assassination of a Presbyterian lord – to put the cat among the pigeons. It would mark the beginning of the King's fightback in the Lowlands. But he did not like such a strategy. It risked too much – MacLeod was a Highlander – it was all right for him. He could disappear into the North if things got too hot in the Lowlands, but his lands lay within twenty miles of Edinburgh. He could not risk any retribution. He might lose everything. He wanted to wait and see what happened in the North. And that is what they would now do. Now that MacLeod was dead. The balance had tipped in favour of caution. MacLeod had been useful for the cause. He was full of energy, perhaps too much. It could not be helped.

He was also worried about the marriage settlement. He needed all the documents signed immediately and Stirling was stalling again. Stirling was a vacillating fool, a bumbling idiot. He needed the money as soon as possible. Two debts had to be redeemed within a month. They could not be rolled over. Two more were due the following month. In addition, he needed cash to fund the King's cause. The promise of French gold had not materialised yet.

Mrs Hair was another thorn in his side. She had trapped him. He was sure she had planned it all. If he did not find cash within a matter of weeks he would lose Longlandrigg, the best piece of land on his estate. How was he – an earl, at the top, or near the top of the Scottish nobility – in thrall to the widow of a druggist! How was the world come to such a pitiful state? It really was a grubby little Revolution that had brought William to the throne. But if the true King returned, the world would be transformed again. The natural order under God would be restored. And he would be rewarded for his loyalty – a Dukedom perhaps! A generous pension and lands of forfeited Presbyterians who would be exiled again! Then all his debts would mean nothing. He would be rich and live like a nobleman again, not like a pathetic little merchant.

The curtain of the snug was pulled back suddenly. David Drummond's avuncular face appeared. Drummond took a seat beside him. He did not trust the grasping lawyer. Drummond acted solely in the interest of Perth and Melfort and no one else. And that pair of rogues could not be trusted. They were partly responsible for the King's troubles in Scotland. One moment Drummond suggested caution; the next violent retribution! How could you trust such a man? How poorly served was the King in this land.

'Good evening, my lord,' said Drummond, removing his hat and bowing deferentially.

'Where are the others?' Dewarton asked impatiently.

'They'll be here soon. Don't worry, my lord. A bottle to share?'

He imagined himself free of the likes of Drummond and Hair and Stirling. A nobleman with power again, loyal to his King, beloved by his true King. The true order of things re-established. His lands free of the curse of debt. The Presbyterian hounds off his back and returned to their pen. Then he would have time to hunt and feast and enjoy himself without worry. He felt anger rising within him. He must calm himself. After all, Gourlay was on his side. Thank God for George Gourlay who had rescued him from a few scrapes over the years. Gourlay was an old friend. He would see him right when the time came. He would do anything for him and would be well rewarded as always.

CHAPTER 17

Discoveries in the Library

ON THE APPROACH to the Hawthorns, MacKenzie's country house, Scougall always remembered his first visit, which had been a few years before. He had been amazed by the splendour of the walled garden in bloom, of the four tall ewe trees on the lawn and, perhaps most of all, of the young woman emerging from the front door to greet them. She was as beautiful a creature as he had ever seen. He would never forget the moment he saw Elizabeth for the first time. He smiled to himself as he recalled his tongue-tied embarrassment. But now she was gone from the house. It grieved him that she would not be there to welcome them. Instead old Meg was at the door, looking slightly annoyed with the world as usual, and a boy, her grandson, preparing to take the horses. Scougall spluttered a couple of mispronounced words of Gaelic in greeting, sending Meg into a fit of laughter. 'Davie Scougall speaking the Gaelic!' she shrieked.

MacKenzie barked orders at her and encouraged Scougall to walk with him in the gardens. They wandered for a while along one of the borders in silence. 'Look here, Davie.' MacKenzie was standing beside a flowering shrub. 'Look at the simple beauty of this flower. I've given my garden little thought because of all this business – Elizabeth and now MacLeod.' Scougall had still not acquired any interest in horticulture, after all he had no garden of his own, but he let MacKenzie drone on about the cultivation of tulips and the problems of roses, nodding now and again to feign interest.

MacKenzie said they should take a glass of wine in the library and, while MacKenzie organised things, Scougall browsed the bookshelves which contained books in Latin, English, French,

Italian and Spanish. He put his hand on the spine of a book randomly and pulled it out. It was *A Description of New England* by John Smith published in London in 1616. For a moment he saw the face of Agnes Morrison and he wondered where in America she was gone, and whether he would ever see her again, but his thoughts were interrupted by MacKenzie who placed a glass of wine in his hand. MacKenzie took a gulp of claret then told him to remove the congealed paper from his pouch. Scougall put the glass down and placed the paper ball on a table at the window where two candles had been lit to aid the examination. MacKenzie took a pair of tweezers and began to tease the sheets apart, like the petals of a pallid flower. Delicate from its soaking, it took a few minutes to disentangle three separate sheets. One was a short letter, the other two were memorandums about four inches by three. The writing on them was almost too small to read. He placed them on the table and smoothed them out carefully. Then, taking up a magnifying glass, he began to read. He saw that the ink was faded and there were dark stains from the water. He looked up at Scougall excitedly: 'I think we have something here, Davie. Have a look yourself.' Scougall took the glass. The first memo listed a series of payments:

1 March 1689 Item payment by AS 100 pounds

1 April 1689 Item payment by AS 100 pounds

1 May 1689 Item payment by AS 100 pounds

1 June 1689 Item payment by AS 100 pounds

1 July 1689 Item payment by AS 100 pounds

'What do you make of it?' asked MacKenzie.

'It looks like a record of payments of 100 pounds by AS at the beginning of each month,' replied Scougall.

'And who is AS?'

Scougall pondered the initials for a few moments. A name came into his mind. 'Adam Scobie?'

'Or Andrew Stein?' suggested MacKenzie.

'Or Abraham Slight, perhaps,' added Scougall.

'Why would any of them be making payments to MacLeod for such large sums?'

Scougall shook his head. 'Could it be the repayment of a debt or... contributions to the Jacobite cause?'

MacKenzie nodded. 'As far as we know, neither Stein, Scobie or Slight are supporters of the old King.'

'So, it might be just a debt, with repayments made each month?'

MacKenzie nodded again, then turned his attention to the second memo. 'What about this one?' Scougall looked at it carefully through the glass. At the top was written faintly *Homines Fidelis*.

'The loyal men,' said Scougall, translating the Latin.

MacKenzie smiled. 'Supporters of King James, most likely.'

Underneath was a series of Latin words running vertically and horizontally with values in Roman numerals arranged thus:

	Capillamentum	Vallum	Bellum	Capillamentum
Comitis	V	V	V	V
Virgilius	II	II	II	II
Argentum	I	I	I	I
Tympanum	I	I	II	I

'It doesn't make any sense to me, sir,' said Scougall.

MacKenzie smiled. 'They're in some kind of cipher, Davie. I would suggest they are Jacobite contacts of MacLeod. It may be a record of attendance at meetings and perhaps financial contributions made by each to the cause.'

'A list of Jacobites?' asked Scougall.

'Precisely. A list of notable Jacobites in the city. With meeting places and the amount provided at each meeting. This is an important discovery, Davie.'

MacKenzie scanned the list again. After a few moments, he turned to Scougall. 'Who is *Tympanum*, Davie?'

'The word is Latin for drum, sir.'

MacKenzie thought for a moment. 'Precisely. Could he be David Drummond?'

'It makes sense, sir,' said Scougall. 'What about *Argentum*? Latin for silver. I cannot think who it could be.'

'Let's come back to that one. What about *Virgilius*?'

'The author of the *Aeneid*, Virgil.'

'Aeneas MacLeod himself?' suggested MacKenzie.

'Yes, sir.'

'And the other, *Comitis*.'

'*Comitis* is Latin for Earl, so likely a nobleman. One of the Jacobite inclined nobles who have remained in town such as Panmure or Dewarton.'

'Good, Davie. What about the meeting places? *Vallum... bellum... capillamentum...*'

Scougall thought for a moment. He was quite skilled in legal Latin from his work as a notary. '*Vallum* is Latin for rampart. Somewhere near a rampart? *Bellum* is war. I'm not sure about *capillamentum*.'

'*Capillamentum* means wig, Davie.'

'Of course. I don't see it too often in my instruments. Could it be the Periwig?'

'It makes sense. If we are right this small group of Jacobites met four times, twice in the Periwig and at two other locations. They raised funds each time. Finally, the letter, Davie. Read it to me.'

Scougall took the magnifying glass again. The letter was dated 10 July 1689. He read slowly in a monotone voice:

> Burn after reading. These are important days for the family. The fox will land soon in the city. Please pass on to *Tympanum*. The news from the country is good. The lion sends presents which will arrive soon. The fox will engage with the goose. The family are ready to act. We await news from the fox and the lion. *Post Scriptum*. I seek money for my own needs. Please issue a

bond for 250 pounds Scots and see the money is
sent north as soon as possible. Your dearest and
affectionate cousin, MacLeod of Dunvegan.

Scougall raised his head. He looked baffled. 'What does it all
mean, sir?'

'It's in code so it cannot be used as evidence if intercepted.
It all seems obvious to me. We should be able to work out who
the characters are. For example, the lion is clearly King James,
the fox is Dundee and MacKay is the goose. I think it might
be a message to Jacobites in Edinburgh. King James intends to
supply soldiers to Dundee's army in the Highlands and they
should prepare to act here in the city. Cause a stir of some kind.'

'A stir, sir?'

'A stir such as an explosion.'

'Do you think MacLeod was responsible for the explosion?'

'This suggests he could've been. I'm not sure. It would be
risky from their point of view. Killing innocent townsfolk as
well as Presbyterians. It's maybe just a warning to be ready. Or
a pointer to do something else?'

'MacLeod did not burn the letter, sir.'

'Perhaps he was killed soon after receiving it.' MacKenzie
looked at the papers again. Deep in thought, he began to pace
round the library. 'We need to put our thinking caps on, Davie.
We need to identify all the loyal men and we need to find the
identity of AS. It might lead us to the killer.'

CHAPTER 18

A Conversation with Daniel Jabb

AFTER BREAKFAST AT the Hawthorns, they returned to Edinburgh. MacKenzie said little on the ride back to town and Scougall was happy with his own thoughts. He recalled that he would have to return to his office to complete a couple of instruments. He would also have to prepare himself for his visit home to Musselburgh, look out his best suit and polish his shoes. He needed to look his best. After returning the horses to the stables in the Cowgate, MacKenzie led Scougall up St Mary's Close. 'Come, Davie. Let's start the morning with a little news. I believe the *Gazette* is published here by Mr Jabb.'

MacKenzie climbed down the stairs into the basement of a tenement and pushed the door open. There were piles of paper everywhere with a printing press taking up most of the space. Jabb was a fair-haired man in his late twenties with a freckled face wearing a dirty purple jacket. He was busy setting type, a look of intense concentration on his face.

'Mr Daniel Jabb?' asked MacKenzie.

Jabb looked up from his type, appearing unperturbed by their arrival. 'What can I do for you gentlemen?' He was used to folk just dropping in to see him.

MacKenzie introduced himself and Scougall. 'May we have a few moments of your time, sir?'

Jabb wiped his hands on a cloth and shook their hands warmly. 'I'm delighted to meet you. I'm sorry for the state of confusion. I'm afraid I can't offer you a seat. There's not enough room,' he laughed.

'What brings you to Scotland, Mr Jabb?' asked MacKenzie. 'Not many of your countrymen venture so far north!'

Jabb laughed again. 'I've been called a strange fish. But I'm a simple man of trade, gentlemen. I'm sure you know London is a great metropolis where all kinds of commodities are bought and sold, including news. There is, however, plenty of competition there. That is not the case in Edinburgh. I was told there was great hunger for news in the city during these days of political change. Only one feeble news sheet is produced by the government. I can do much better than that rubbish, I thought when I read it. I came north last year at the time of the Revolution. I found the place to my liking and I decided to stay for now.'

'For now?' asked Scougall, taken by Jabb's relaxed confidence.

'I aim to establish the paper on a firm footing. Then I'll pass its management on to another while I retain a share of profits. I'll set up another paper in a different location. At least that's my plan. I'll be here for a few months yet.' Scougall reflected that he would like to write something for a news sheet some time, something entirely different from the dry legal documents he churned out day after day.

'The *Gazette* sells well, Mr Jabb?' asked MacKenzie.

'Very well, sir. I'm rushed off my feet, as you see. There are not enough minutes in the day. I write. I set type. I source news. I print. I distribute the paper. I do it all myself. I work day and night. I need an assistant but I've not found one yet. It's a difficult trade. Few are used to it. Now, what can I do for you? Do you want an advertisement in the next issue or do you have a story you would like published? Or do you have some intelligence on something my readers would find interesting? The recent explosion in the Canongate, for example?'

'No, Mr Jabb. We come on other business,' said MacKenzie. 'The business of murder.'

'I see, gentlemen,' replied Jabb, wiping his hands again, clearly interested by what they had to say. 'We're investigating the killing of Aeneas MacLeod,' continued MacKenzie. 'A couple of short pieces mentioning his death have appeared in your paper. I wanted to ask a few questions.'

'Ask away, sir. But remember I may not be able to reveal everything. I must protect my sources. If everything was known, why would anyone buy a paper to find out more? I've built up good contacts already, in a matter of months.'

Nodding to show he respected Jabb's position, MacKenzie asked, 'You claim MacLeod was a well-known supporter of the old King. Indeed, you imply he was killed for this reason.'

Jabb smiled. 'Ah, politics, politics. That's what I believe, sir. I didn't say it explicitly in the *Gazette*, if you read my words closely. I said it was claimed by some on the street he was killed for this reason. I don't know for certain if it's the case. But I would say, many people in the city believe it.'

'Do you know anything of the man or men who carried out the killing?'

'Nothing, sir. If I knew anything definite myself, I'd report it to the Advocate. If I had any strong hints I would publish them in the *Gazette* to flush out the killer or killers.'

'What do you think happened to MacLeod, Mr Jabb?' asked Scougall, taking out his notebook and pencil.

'Let me tell you what I think, gentlemen. MacLeod was a young man who held strong political opinions. No one will argue with that. There are many men like him on both sides of the political divide. He was known to be fundraising for the old King. I believe no one would deny he was a Jacobite. Others are not as active in their support for the old King. The government viewed him as a danger. I know they were keeping a close eye on him.'

'What do you mean, keeping a close eye on?' asked MacKenzie.

'I mean he was being followed by one of their spies. You should ask Dalrymple about MacLeod. Whatever the case, someone decided to get rid of him. I don't know where the order came from. If it was from the government, Dalrymple for example who gave the order, or from the Presbyterian leadership or, perhaps, another Jacobite.'

'Why would another Jacobite kill him?' asked Scougall, confused.

'Such movements are driven by jealousies, different competing factions. One is favoured and another is not. A man as young as MacLeod was favoured and perhaps another hated him for it. Do you follow me?'

MacKenzie nodded, then asked. 'So you're convinced it was a political killing?'

'I've heard MacLeod described as a crucial figure in Jacobite circles. He was close to agents of the old King and, through his clan, to an important chief, who is believed to support James. Removing MacLeod makes sense from the government's point of view. Political assassination is not, of course, without risk.'

'It's been suggested that his connection with Mrs Hair was important.'

'I know nothing about her involvement. It seems a bit far-fetched to me. An old woman conspiring to kill one of her own writers? It would make good copy in the *Gazette*, but I think it unlikely. I would not publish such a story unless I had real evidence.'

'I meant rather, MacLeod was killed as a way of getting at Mrs Hair.'

'Was he that important to her?' asked Jabb, looking interested.

'I don't know, Mr Jabb. Is there anything else, not yet published in your paper, that you might have heard?' MacKenzie was sure that Jabb was not telling them all he knew.

'I may have something small, but you'll have to wait for the next edition.' Jabb replied, smiling ruefully.

'Could you not be persuaded to share it with us just now?'

'I publish at the end of the week.' Jabb wiped his hands again on the rag. He rose then sat back again on the edge of his desk. 'But I can see you'll not blab all over town so I'll tell you this. I know MacLeod was being followed by a spy.'

'You have said that already, sir.'

'I know that spy goes by the name of 'KYLE'.' He spelt out the name for them. 'That's not his name but what he's referred to in communications.'

'Who do you think he is?' asked Scougall eagerly. He thought hard – he knew that 'Kyle' was an area in the west, part of Ayrshire.

'I've no idea, Mr Scougall. You should ask the Advocate. He's responsible for him. I do know he was spying on MacLeod for a number of weeks before he was killed.'

'Then it's possible he could be the killer or know what happened to MacLeod?' asked MacKenzie.

'That's entirely possible, sir.'

MacKenzie was pleased by the discovery. They were making progress at last. He decided to move on to another matter. 'Do you think the explosion is connected to a struggle between Gourlay and Stein for influence in the city?'

Jabb shook his head. 'I don't believe so. I think the Jacobites were behind it. They aimed to damage the government by destabilising the city, adding a little terror to the mix. They pray Dundee is successful in the Highlands. The more they hurt the Whig interest here, the better. In my experience, struggles between men like Gourlay and Stein are not fought out so publicly. The explosion has a whiff of symbolism about it. It reminds me of the powder plot which almost killed James's grandfather. Jacobites love such things.'

'Thank you for sharing this with us, Mr Jabb. You've been very helpful.' MacKenzie turned towards the door, 'Come, Davie. We've taken up enough of Mr Jabb's time.' But he halted on the way out. 'It's said you also are in the pay of the government, Mr Jabb. You're a spy like Kyle. Are you Kyle?'

Jabb laughed. 'If that was the case I wouldn't be struggling here alone. I'd employ someone to do this work and spend my time sniffing out stories in taverns, rather than typesetting. That's where I'd like to spend my time if I could afford to, that's where the best copy is obtained. I've no time to be Kyle, Mr MacKenzie.'

'And do you know Gourlay?'

'I've met him a couple of times. I know his reputation. He's getting old. The other fish in the pond sense his decline. They smell his weakness.'

'And Captain Andrew Stein?'

'Stein is ambitious. I've met him once. He told me to stop asking his men for stories. But they will take a drink from anyone.'

'Is Stein stepping on Gourlay's toes?'

'I believe you could say that.'

'But you've published nothing in the *Gazette* about their rivalry?'

'I must be careful, gentlemen. I don't want to make enemies as a newcomer to town. Gourlay still has power in the city. Even working here in this tenement, I must make a small contribution to him. Stein may soon have power.'

'How are your relations with the Advocate?'

Again, he smiled. 'I thought you were leaving. I work for myself, Mr MacKenzie, if that's what you imply. I'm a man of independent means. I only receive money from the sale of the paper and advertisements placed in it. Nothing comes from the government. If I took Dalrymple's fee, he would dictate what I write, resulting in a dull publication which no one would buy. Rather, the people clamour for the next edition of my *Gazette*. People want to read something of interest. They desire stories about the rich and famous, salacious copy about noblemen's daughters and the debauchery of ministers. That's what sells papers. They don't want a dull tract outlining the government's religious policy. When I have a story, one which looks bad for the government, if Dalrymple is caught with his trousers down in a bawdy house, I'll publish. I hold my independence above all things and the people love me for that.'

'I am glad of it, Mr Jabb. I look forward to the next edition,' said Mackenzie turning and raising his pipe in farewell.

CHAPTER 19

The Apartments of Betty McGrain

AFTER LEAVING JABB's they headed for Watson's Wynd further up the High Street where Galbraith had told them Betty McGrain lived in an apartment on the fourth storey of a tenement. There was no answer when MacKenzie knocked on the door. He waited a few moments and knocked again. They heard a noise inside. Another minute then the door opened slightly. A single, distrustful eye could be seen behind it.

Scougall moved forward and looked in. 'It's Mr Scougall, Betty. We spoke in Mrs Hair's office. I've brought my friend Mr MacKenzie to speak to you. He would like to ask you more about Mr MacLeod.'

The door opened a bit further. The eye scanned them both suspiciously.

'I see you're scared, my dear,' said MacKenzie reassuringly. 'There's no need to be. We only want to ask a few questions. We won't take up much of your time.'

'I don't want to speak of him!' she snapped.

'It's very important, Betty. Mrs Hair has told us that you would speak about it.'

The eye withdrew into the darkness. There was silence for a few moments. Then the door opened and she stood back, allowing them inside. They followed her down a short passageway to a bright living chamber. It was a compact suite of rooms, neatly furnished with a kitchen and bedchamber off the main room.

'I don't have visitors, often. I don't like it,' she said coldly, walking towards the windows to look down on the High

Street. She stood nervously, dressed plainly in a black skirt and white bonnet, looking unhappy with the world.

'This is a pleasant place you have here, Miss McGrain. Have you stayed here long?' asked MacKenzie affably, surveying the tidy interior.

'Since I came to town.'

'When was that, my dear?'

'About a year ago.'

'Where did you come from?'

'I was raised in the town of Stirling.' Her answers were short and not encouraging.

'Ah, Stirling is a fine town. I've a few clients there myself. You might know Mr MacDougall, a merchant in Gracie's Wynd, and Peter Hay in Stobbie's Close?'

She shook her head vacantly.

'Many Highlanders have made a home there,' continued MacKenzie. 'Being so close to the Highlands, it's a good base for the droving trade.' He glanced around the room. 'May we sit?' She nodded. There was a narrow couch in the centre of the chamber. She remained at the window, arms crossed defensively over her chest, a frown on her face. 'I'm investigating the death of Aeneas MacLeod,' MacKenzie continued, 'as I'm sure Mr Scougall has already explained. Could you tell me what happened between you, Miss McGrain?'

'Between us?' she repeated in disbelief. Anger flashed across her face. 'Nothing happened between us! I didn't seek his company. He accosted me. My life is much improved by his demise!'

'He sought you out in the office?' asked MacKenzie.

'Yes. I've told him already about it all,' she nodded angrily at Scougall. 'MacLeod fondled me roughly in the office. He then assaulted me in a vennel. Held me by the neck. Said vile things to me. Said he would have me by force if I resisted. Said he would kill me. He was a drunken sot. And then it happened again in the office.'

'He said he would kill you?' asked MacKenzie.

'Yes. He said something like that, if I didn't do what he wanted. He threatened me with violence… he was a… I hated him.'

'I'm sorry you've suffered so much at his hands. Could you tell us what you can remember? It would be a great help.'

She turned to look out the window and spoke as she gazed down on the High Street. 'He was pleasant enough at first but suddenly turned, as if possessed by an evil spirit.'

'Did he say he would kill you?'

She thought for a moment. 'He hinted something bad would happen to me if I resisted him.'

'I understand, Miss McGrain. The more we learn about him, the less liking we have for him. But we must find out the truth about his death. Every man and woman deserves that, even the worst sinner. You were angry about the way he treated you and the things he said, is that correct?'

'It is, sir.' She appeared to thaw slightly. She turned back towards them, but remained beside the window.

'You went to see Mrs Hair about him, seeking her help?'

'I did. She listened to me. She believed me. She told me she would put a stop to it. I believe she spoke to him about it. It did stop, for a while. He didn't come near me for weeks. I thought he was done with me. I began to forget him. I was able to come to the office again without fear in my heart.'

'Then it started again?'

'A few weeks later, I was walking home. He grabbed me by the neck in a vennel and threatened me. Then he approached me again in the kitchen.'

MacKenzie moved forward in his seat and his tone suddenly changed. He wanted to catch her off-guard. 'Did you have to take things into your own hands, Betty,' he said sternly, raising his voice. 'You decided to get rid of him. Is that what happened?'

She hesitated again. 'No, sir. I didn't do anything to him. I'd never do such a thing. It was not me. I did not kill him! I wasn't sorry when I heard he was dead. I'm not sorry he's dead, God forgive me. He would have abused other women for the rest of his days. I know that for certain. He was a servant of the Devil!' she screamed, becoming animated.

'You were seen threatening him with a knife, not long before he disappeared. You were seen by Mr Farquharson in the kitchen, saying you would use it on him if he came near you again,' continued MacKenzie. Scougall squirmed. He knew MacKenzie's tactics could be effective but could never do anything like that himself. She turned to look out the window again. Her head dropped. When she turned back, there were tears on her cheeks.

She spoke in a whisper. 'He said he would... he said he would follow me... he called me whore and harlot. He swore and cursed at me. He said he would seek me out wherever I went. I didn't know what I should do. He said he would follow me and take me. So, I took a knife from the table in the kitchen. I threatened him with it. I screamed I would kill him if he came near me again. I lost my senses I was so scared. But I swear. I did not kill him. I would never kill any creature. It would go against the Lord's Commandments. I knew he was the Devil's spawn. The spawn of Satan. I knew I had to fight him, but not by killing him. I would fight him in other ways. Fight him with prayer and by reforming myself, by making myself free from sin. I prayed to the Lord for some hint about what I should do to be rid of him, but there was no answer from Him. Then MacLeod disappeared. A few days later I heard he was killed. It was as if God answered my prayers. It was divine justice. But I swear I did not kill him. If he treated others as he treated me, he would have many enemies. I'm not surprised he met such an end.' She broke down, leaning against the wall and bursting into sobs.

MacKenzie rose to comfort her. He took her by the arm and gently helped her into a chair. 'I'm sorry, my dear. I'm sorry for asking so many questions. But I need to find out the truth. Now, tell me everything you know, every last thing. Tell me the first time you met him and your first impressions of him.'

She sat on a chair opposite them and spoke vacantly staring ahead at the wall opposite, not meeting their eyes. 'I first met him in July 1688, so about a year ago, when I started in the office.' She went on to recount her dealings with MacLeod which she had already told Scougall. MacKenzie nodded now and again, listening intently. 'He told me Mrs Hair would soon be dead and he would run the office. The office would be his. Then I would have to do his bidding. I would serve him as his whore. It was then I took up a knife lying on the table. I swear I did not kill him.'

'He said Mrs Hair would soon be dead, you're sure of it?' asked MacKenzie.

'Yes. He said it in her own kitchen. It angered me so much. She's been so good to me. She's a kind soul, although few know it. She's hated for no reason other than she's a woman.' MacKenzie watched her carefully. Her expression reminded him of someone else but he could not recall who it was.

'Is there anything more you can tell us about him, Betty? What about his friends and colleagues?'

'I had nothing to do with him outside the office. If I saw him on the street, I went the other way. Once I saw him in the company of Dewarton. At the time, I didn't know who it was, but Billy Farquharson who was walking with me recognised the earl. I learned later he was a notorious Jacobite. MacLeod was deep in conversation with him.'

MacKenzie got to his feet and Scougall followed. 'Thank you, Betty. That's all for now, my dear. We'll not trouble you further today. It's the lawyer's curse – I must represent both good and bad clients. MacLeod was a bad one. But his family demands justice, you must understand. It's important for the MacLeod clan. I'm sure you're relieved by his demise and I can understand why. Some men believe they can demand everything from a woman. Some go through life destroying the lives of others.' MacKenzie thought of Ruairidh MacKenzie and his daughter, and anger flushed through him.

On the way down the stairs, he stopped Scougall. 'Do you believe her, Davie?'

Scougall was surprised by the question. There was no doubt in his mind she was telling the truth. 'I believe her completely, sir. How could she pretend like that? How could she act out all that? You saw the fear on her face.'

'I think you're right. But there's something that doesn't quite fit. A servant in the service of Mrs Hair living in comfort in a fine suite of rooms with books and good furniture? Something's amiss. But she has, however, provided us with the identity of another of the loyal men.'

'Dewarton?' suggested Scougall.

'Yes. I think Dewarton is *comitis*.'

CHAPTER 20

The Writing Booth of Adam Scobie

SCOUGALL LOVED THE Luckenbooths, the warren of tiny shops and stalls surrounding St Giles Kirk. It was a noisy bustling place during office hours where you could buy anything under the sun. He would often spend an hour rummaging for a bargain, a new book or golf club. It was also where writers rented booths to run their businesses from. Scobie's booth was at the end of a row, against the wall of the church. Its position indicated that business was not good, rents were lowest there and it was clear that he had sunk to the bottom of his profession. Scougall thanked God he could afford the basement of a tenement on the High Street. A booth was stuffy in the summer and freezing in winter. It also provided little privacy. Those clients wanting confidentiality would go elsewhere.

MacKenzie rapped on the tarpaulin with his stick. Almost immediately the head of a young man popped out. When Scobie saw he was being visited by members of his own profession, his face lit up, and he swung open the cloth, beckoning them inside. There was only a tiny wooden desk and a couple of ill-made, wooden stools inside.

'What can I do for you, gentlemen?' began Scobie, excitedly. 'An instrument quickly and accurately written, at a slight discount to official rates, or a letter in a clear and polished hand or a bond perhaps? I can deliver anything by close of business today. I trained with John MacGregor, Writer to the Signet.'

'I'm sorry, Mr Scobie,' began MacKenzie. 'Our business is of a different nature. If I may shut the... door, please.' MacKenzie drew the tarpaulin back across the opening to Scobie's booth.

'Of course, take a stool, sir. I must apologise for my humble abode.' Scobie offered Scougall the stool behind his desk but he declined preferring to stand. 'You are Davie Scougall, sir? I know you. You are well-regarded in our profession. And you must be Mr MacKenzie, the advocate. I'm honoured, sir. I take on work of any kind, no matter how small, anything.' Scobie smiled nervously, emphasising the last word. There was a hungry look about him. He was clearly desperate for new business. 'I'm sorry I've nothing to offer as refreshments. The uncertainty of the times... you will know it well, Mr MacKenzie.'

'Thank you, Mr Scobie. If it's okay with you, I'll get straight to the point.' MacKenzie lowered himself carefully onto the small stool. 'We're concerned with a criminal case. We represent the kin of someone you are acquainted with... the kin of Aeneas MacLeod.'

Scobie's demeanour altered. The friendliness disappeared. He stiffened his back and his face darkened. 'What's MacLeod got to do with me?' he asked coldly.

'We're investigating his death for his family. The clan MacLeod are disappointed with the progress of official investigations by the Advocate. They want to know why he was killed and who is responsible. The Advocate is too busy with political business. We've already visited Mrs Hair's office. We were told about an altercation you had with MacLeod a few months ago.'

'I had to leave that place. I could not stand it any longer, sir.'

'Tell us why, Mr Scobie.'

Scobie closed his eyes and offered a short prayer in a whisper. He opened them again and raised his head. 'MacLeod was a despicable creature. He was an irreligious fiend. He mocked everything holy in this world and the next one. He decried everything of goodness and purity. He was a truly horrid blasphemer.'

'A blasphemer?' repeated Scougall, trying awkwardly to record Scobie's words while standing up.

'I believe he was an atheist and a Sadducee,' continued Scobie. 'He declaimed the spirit world as preposterous. From the start of my time in the office he mocked me. He mocked everything about me: my dress, voice, family. He mocked the Covenanting folk of Ayrshire and finally he mocked my religion. I tried to reply to his jokes with scorn but his tongue was too sharp. He always had a riposte which caused hilarity in the office, whether mimicking the ministers or criticising the government. It was obvious he favoured the old King. The last straw was the stupid etchings.'

MacKenzie took out his pipe and gave it a knock on the corner of the desk to remove the ash. 'Do you mind?' Before Scobie could answer he was lighting his pipe. 'Please, continue.'

Scobie did not look pleased as MacKenzie began to puff away filling the booth with smoke. 'When I decried them, he left them pinned to my desk. I know it was to annoy me. No, it was to hurt me. I believe his aim was to drive me from the office and he was successful. I lost control of myself, which I regret. I attacked him in the office. I was foolish. But I could not help it. It was schoolyard stuff. I landed a punch on his cheek. He struck me back. After a few punches, we were pulled apart. We had more words in a tavern later that night. I challenged him to a duel. He refused, laughing at me again.'

MacKenzie pondered for a few moments, observing the young writer carefully, before asking: 'Did you ever threaten his life, Mr Scobie?'

Scobie shook his head. 'I challenged him to a duel, as I said. Many heard me doing so in the tavern. It was the honourable thing to do. I wouldn't kill him in cold blood. I would only kill justly, in the proper way, man to man.'

MacKenzie adjusted his position on the stool, painfully. He needed to get on with this. 'You were heard saying you would kill him during the fight in the office. Did you lose control? Did you seek him out? Did you use your knife to slit his throat? Did you have his body dumped in a cold pit?'

Scobie shook his head again. There were beads of sweat on his brow. He looked forlorn. 'No, sir. I swear. I swear on the good Book. I swear on God Almighty's own words. I would never kill like that. I admit I was angry with him. I thought of killing him. I dreamed of doing it. I desired it in my heart. I despised him.'

'You have a clear motive, Mr Scobie.'

'I believed he was the servant of Antichrist. He was a friend of Papists. An acolyte of Satan. But I did not kill him. I would never sin like that. I would never sin so grossly. I had no choice but to leave the office. I couldn't work in his company any longer. MacLeod was a knave. He cared for nothing but himself. He got what was coming to him, if you ask me. God intervened. Many people hated him. He was arrogant. He boasted of women he'd bedded and the money he made from illicit deals. I don't know why she employed him. But I swear, I did not kill him.'

Scobie was shaking when he finished his rant. He was sitting forward on the edge of his stool, rocking back and forwards slightly. There were tears in his eyes. Scougall thought that he looked on the verge of breaking down completely. 'Do you have any idea who did kill him, Mr Scobie?' asked Scougall, feeling sorry for the condition MacKenzie's questions had brought him to. MacKenzie appeared unperturbed, staring intently at him.

'He kept grotesque company.'

'Who do you refer to?' asked MacKenzie.

'I saw him with the scum of this city. Jacobites like Drummond and Dewarton. I saw him with men like Gourlay, a known degenerate, who live off the earnings of vice and debauchery. He was thick with the like of them.'

'Where did you see him with them?'

'I saw him with Gourlay a number of times in taverns. I saw him with Dewarton on the street and in coffee houses. He boasted about it in the office. How he was entertained by an earl. How he would marry an earl's daughter himself one day.'

And then MacKenzie relaxed. He sat back and smiled, the tone of his voice softening. 'Was there anything particular he was working on before his disappearance?' he asked as if he was speaking to a colleague in the law.

Scobie closed his eyes. He let out a sigh. He was relieved to be free of MacKenzie's intense gaze. 'I think he was examining debts of Fraser of Lovat.'

'What was the manner of the work?'

'Mrs Hair was thinking of buying them. She wanted to know the quality of the estates, how productive they were, the division between Highland and Lowland pasture, the kind of crops grown and the yields, if there was room for improving rents, how difficult it was to transport deals and cattle from the Highlands, what price was reasonable for wadsets and other debts – those kinds of question.' Scobie also relaxed and his demeanour appeared less feverish.

'Why was she so interested in Lovat's debts?' asked Scougall. He knew that the Frasers of Lovat were a Jacobite clan.

'I don't know, sir. Perhaps it was an insurance policy in case the Jacobites are successful. If King James reclaims his throne, the chiefs who support him, like Lovat, will prosper. The price of their debts will rise too. She has little to do with the Highlands usually, but I overheard her saying to him she wanted to extend her business there. She will even benefit from the whiff of a Jacobite Restoration.'

'What do you mean by a whiff of a restoration?' asked MacKenzie, confused.

'It will not matter if James does return to his throne. The fear of a restoration will push up the price of Lovat's bonds and those of other Jacobite chiefs.'

'I see. She's a canny operator indeed, Mr Scobie,' said MacKenzie rising painfully. 'And where do you hail from yourself?'

'I was born and bred in Ayrshire, sir. My father is the miller at Mackieston Mill on the River Ayr. It's a bonnie spot. I wish I could return to live there, but how could a writer earn a living?'

'The nobles employ notaries in their households, Mr Scobie,' added Scougall. He had once thought about taking a position himself in the household of the Earl of Tweeddale.

'I know, sir. But I must find one who shares my own viewpoint on religion. I do not like the degeneracy of some of the Scottish noblemen.'

Scougall agreed with Scobie. He would hate to be enslaved in the household of an arrogant laird or lord. Better to be a free man in a miserable booth, he reflected, as he followed MacKenzie out.

CHAPTER 21

An Audience with the Advocate

IN THE AFTERNOON MacKenzie went alone to Parliament House behind St Giles Kirk. He had arranged a meeting with the Lord Advocate. Scougall had gone home to Musselburgh for a few hours to meet Christina Munro, a possible marriage candidate invited to the house by his mother. Dalrymple sat behind a huge, ancient desk of black wood in the candlelit chamber. On the panelled walls were portraits of previous incumbents of the country's highest legal office. MacKenzie sat opposite him recalling the many times he had sat in the chamber when his kinsman George MacKenzie of Rosehaugh was Lord Advocate. Now Rosehaugh was gone from the scene. Despite being a slippery character, he missed him. The new incumbent Dalrymple was a different man entirely. A Whig and Lowlander through and through, he was the son of the jurist James Dalrymple, elevated as President of the Session since the Revolution. Father and son were known to be inveterate haters of all things relating to the Gaelic-speaking areas of Scotland.

Dalrymple looked up from a letter he was writing. His long, pale face was joyless. 'I have so much correspondence. I must write to the King in London every day. He wants informed about everything in Scotland. All the goings-on in this nation. How are you, MacKenzie?'

'As well as can be expected sir, thank you.'

'It must be difficult to be back here without him. I believe you were close to... bloody MacKenzie.'

MacKenzie did not respond to Dalrymple's description of his kinsman. He had reverted to the role he was used to, that of advocate, and he remained completely calm. 'He did his best in difficult circumstances, my lord. Perhaps, as you hint, he was too prone to the use of force against the Presbyterians. I agree that force is rarely a solution to thorny, political problems.'

'I'm a busy man, MacKenzie. What can I do for you today?' Dalrymple looked down at the letter in front of him again and took up his quill. He wrote a few words and raised his head. MacKenzie knew he wanted to give the impression he was too busy to bother with another minor MacKenzie.

'Thank you for seeing me at such short notice, my lord. I'm here in a private capacity. I represent the kin of Aeneas MacLeod of Rhenigidale in Harris, the young writer recently slain whose body was found at Craigleith.'

Dalrymple sat back in his seat and put his quill down. As he spoke there was the hint of a sly smile on his lips. 'The MacLeods are a nest of thieves, MacKenzie. Almost as bad as the clan MacDonald of Glencoe who are a tribe of lawless barbarians! They deserve to be run out of this land. The MacDonalds have no love of the law of this nation. They steal and burn and cause mayhem. Now they help the rebel Dundee. The MacLeods are little better, although perhaps more cautious than the Glencoe men. I'm driven to distraction by it all. A rebel army in the Highlands and Jacobites planning God knows what in this city, day after day, night after night. Tell me this, MacKenzie. Why do they seek the return of a fool like James Stuart?'

'A fool, perhaps, my lord. But many believe he's the rightful king of this kingdom. Removing a king by force results in bitter divisions. It's an uncertain time for us all. But I'm not here on a political matter. I don't hold strong opinions either way on the worthiness of James Stuart. I'm only concerned with the murder of Aeneas MacLeod. The killing was an unlawful act. His throat was cut. He received dishonourable burial. I intend to get to the bottom of it.'

'You say you are no Jacobite, MacKenzie.' Dalrymple rummaged on his desk and pulled out a sheet of paper which he held up. 'But I have good intelligence that your own chief Seaforth sups with James in Ireland as we speak. Many of your kinsmen are plotting his return! Many MacKenzies are in the hills with Dundee in open rebellion. I've heard it said your own daughter is with the Jacobite army in the Highlands.'

MacKenzie conquered the anger in his soul when he heard this. He knew Dalrymple would use anything to get under your skin and make you lose control. 'I've an argument with my chief on a private matter, my lord. Leave my daughter out of this. I don't follow Seaforth in politics or religion. I prefer to sit out this disagreement. I observe events, only. I'm not involved in them.' He was pleased with himself for remaining calm.

'You would be advised to continue to take such a position. King William will win in the end, no matter how good a general leads that rabble in the Highlands. William has the backing of the merchants of Amsterdam. They have more gold than Midas. James is supported by a few bankrupt chiefs and their savage retainers.'

'What about Aeneas MacLeod's activity in support of James, my lord?'

Dalrymple was silent for a few moments before replying. 'I know MacLeod was connected to unsavoury elements in this city... both criminal... and political ones.'

'What do you mean exactly, my lord?

'MacLeod was trying to raise protection money from certain shopkeepers in the Cowgate. He was only a young writer for God's sake! How does a notary diversify into such business! He was often seen in the company of rogues and reprobates. On the political front, he drank often with Dewarton, a well-known supporter of the Stuart, and the advocate David Drummond, lackey of the Drummond brothers. This nation is surely better off without him!'

'But he was not tried by a court of law, sir,' replied MacKenzie firmly.

'Indeed. Indeed. It's regrettable that he was not. I am a lawyer after all. It would've been better if the law had had its way with him. But it often catches up with such men in other ways. Tell me this MacKenzie. Does the law run in the Highlands which spawned him?'

'I believe it does. The chiefs follow the law as far as circumstances allow them. The power of the government hardly reaches the Highlands, so they must defend themselves. The trouble comes from men who belong to no clan, my lord. And a few clans, through desperation or hunger, are attracted by the old ways of feuding and cattle stealing. However, the Highlands are much changed in the last couple of generations, changed for the better.'

'I wish that was true, MacKenzie,' Dalrymple sighed. 'The Highlands are the heart of my problems. The chiefs must be taught a lesson. It will be a harsh one.'

'I'm not long returned from the north myself. Improvements are being made in farming across eastern Ross-shire and the Black Isle. The chiefs there, MacKenzie cadets, Rosses and Munros do not want war. It's hotheads like Lochiel and Glengarry who have issued the fiery cross, seeing an opportunity to dig themselves out of poverty. But their loyalty can be bought, I'm sure of it. Money will go a long way in the Rough Bounds. Money will solve your Highland problem, not bloody vengeance, my lord. Negotiate with the chiefs. Offer them something concrete.'

'You may be right, MacKenzie. I'll tell you this. MacLeod was supping with the Devil. He perhaps got mauled by one of his companions.'

MacKenzie paused for a moment, before leaning forward in his seat to whisper: 'Was he dispatched by... was he dispatched by King William's government, my lord?'

Dalrymple looked sharply at him. 'I do not sanction assassination, sir. I assure you, the order did not come from this office. MacLeod has annoyed some reprobate. His death bears all the marks of such a killing. Speak to Gourlay or one of the other thugs who infect this city. One day I'll bring them low. Edinburgh will be cleansed of their dirt and the nation of Scotland too. The law will be applied to all citizens from Galloway to Caithness, and that includes the MacDonalds of Glencoe. But first we must win the war. Dundee must be crushed and the rebel clans brought to book.'

MacKenzie sat back in his chair and took out his pipe. 'Was MacLeod under surveillance as a suspected Jacobite?'

Dalrymple thought for a moment before replying. 'Have you ever been in exile, MacKenzie?'

'I haven't, thankfully, my lord,' said MacKenzie, lighting his pipe and blowing clouds of smoke over the desk.

'Well, I can tell you it's an awful thing for a family. We thought we had lost everything built up over a hundred years. All the Dalrymple lands in Ayrshire and the Lothians were given to Papists by a useless King. But, God be praised, through the Lord's intervention our estates are all restored to us. My father is returned as Lord President and I am raised to be Advocate and, perhaps, a higher appointment awaits me. God showed us a vision of Hell, but he has led us back to the promised land. We intend to stay permanently this time. The Dalrymples will not be returning to a Dutch hovel. We will fight tooth and nail to keep our patrimony. I'll do anything in my power to destroy the forces seeking to undermine our glorious revolution. If that includes keeping a close eye on a few enthusiastic Jacobites, by God, I'll do it!' Dalrymple became more animated as he continued. 'There are spies in my employ on the streets. They do an important job for the King's interest. If I gain intelligence of an insurgency here, I'll cut down the Jacobite leaders. But I repeat this to you, MacKenzie. I did not sanction the killing of Aeneas MacLeod.'

'But he was being followed, my lord?'

Dalrymple nodded.

'Does your list of suspects include myself and my friend Archibald Stirling?'

A cold smile lingered on Dalrymple's face. 'As a member of a recalcitrant clan led by a Papist, you were under suspicion, like all MacKenzies.'

'I was under suspicion?'

Dalrymple placed his palm on a pile of documents and gave it a pat with his skeletal hand. 'Reports inform me you are not actively involved in the cause. You are no longer regarded as a prime suspect. I've taken my man off your tail, for now.'

'I'm pleased to hear it your lordship. What about Stirling?'

'Stirling is more of an enthusiast than you but he's absorbed with his daughter's marriage at the moment.'

'Can you tell me who was spying on MacLeod? He might be able to tell us something about his death.'

Dalrymple put an elbow on the desk and held his chin in his hand. 'I can't tell you. It's a matter of state security. I cannot divulge the identity of any of those involved in this kind of work. It could jeopardise their lives.'

'You cannot tell me the identity of...' MacKenzie broke off for a moment to emphasise what followed. 'A man called Kyle.'

'Who told you of him?' Dalrymple snapped.

'I, too, am not at liberty to say, my lord.'

Dalrymple held a quill between his hands and bent it until it snapped. 'Tread carefully, MacKenzie. I'll do anything to preserve the revolution. I would have ordered the killing of MacLeod if I thought it was necessary. I did not think it necessary.'

MacKenzie did not know whether to believe him. He knew Dalrymple could lie all day long if his interest was threatened. He decided to move the interview on to another subject. 'What about the explosion in the Canongate. You had no intelligence of it?'

'I'll tell you what I know about it. The explosion was not planned by Jacobites.'

'Then who was behind it?'

'I do not know. But it had nothing to do with the broader war. I'm sure of that. Now, I must bid you good night. I've work to do, letters to write to the King.' Dalrymple sat back in his seat and held his hand open indicating MacKenzie should take his leave. The audience was over.

'Just one final thing, my lord,' asked MacKenzie as he rose. He had held the question back to last. 'You said you thought my daughter was with Dundee's Highland army.'

Dalrymple nodded. 'I've heard she's in the train of the army with the women.'

MacKenzie shut his eyes for a moment and sucked strongly on his pipe. 'That's not the kind of news a father wants to hear, my lord.' He felt his heart thudding against his chest. He had known it was possible she was with Dundee's army, but confirmation she was at the centre of the bloody struggle in the hills was painful news.

CHAPTER 22

An Unexpected Visitor

MACKENZIE RETURNED TO his study in Libberton's Wynd and sat in his favourite armchair trying not to think about Elizabeth. He tried to focus on the case, in particular the papers found on MacLeod. They were at least making progress. *Comitis* was Dewarton, *Tympanum* Drummond, *Virgil* MacLeod, but who was *Argentum*? And who was AS? – Adam Scobie, Andrew Stein, Abraham Slight or someone else? Was Scobie in debt to MacLeod? Had he decided to kill him because he could not repay it? Or was there some relationship between Stein and MacLeod, a business partnership which had soured. 'Did you find out anything about Slight, Davie?' he asked, turning to Scougall, who sat by the fire having returned from Musselburgh. He was not thinking of MacLeod. His mind was full of Christina Munro. He smiled to himself. He was surprised to have found he liked her. They had only met briefly and taken a short walk down the street. But there was something about her. She teased him gently and she was a bonnie thing. His mother was delighted to hear he liked her. She would arrange another meeting as soon as possible, better not to wait with these things. Better to get on with it, she said. They could go for a longer walk along the shore and eat a meal with the family back at the house. He would see how he felt after a second meeting. Maybe she was the one. Maybe God had tested him, tempting him with Agnes and Elizabeth, lassies above him, when a good Musselburgh match was just right. Then, as often happened after a happy thought, doubt entered his heart. He had neglected to think what she might think of him. A feeling of self-loathing rose in his soul. His face burned red. He had always felt inadequate since he was a bairn. There was something about him that had made the other children bully him. He had always wanted to be one of the crowd in the schoolyard but he was often left alone, daft Davie Scougall. It was a relief to leave for Edinburgh at fourteen and apply himself to legal documents. So how could Christina like him? It was quite possible she thought nothing for him, even despised him as a dull clerk. He closed his eyes and prayed to God she looked kindly on him. At least he had the refuge of his religion. It was the place he had always sought when he felt alone. When he opened them, he found himself staring at the portrait of MacKenzie's wife on the wall. There was such a striking resemblance to her daughter. There was still no word about Elizabeth. The moment of self-hatred passed. He gained his composure. What did it matter about Christina anyway? He hardly knew her. His mother knew plenty of other families in Musselburgh who had eligible daughters.

'Abraham Slight, Davie?' repeated MacKenzie, annoyed that he was being ignored. 'Are you going deaf, man?'

'Sorry, sir. I was lost for a moment.' Scougall sat up, shaking himself out of his reverie. 'Slight was a true believer, sir... he was viewed as an honourable merchant... As steady a Presbyterian as you'll find in Scotland. He's viewed as an honourable merchant by everyone I spoke to. The notion he was connected to MacLeod laughed at as preposterous. He was also rich, sir. His testament proves it. Why would he be paying MacLeod money?'

'Blackmail?'

Scougall nodded. 'I suppose that's possible.'

'Have you had any more thoughts about *Argentum*?'

'There's a notary called John Silver in the next tenement to my office. I believe he tends towards the old King.'

'You might learn what you can about him. How many Silvers or Silvermans can there be in Edinburgh. A handful?' There was a knock on the door. Archie entered and spoke in Gaelic. MacKenzie rose from his chair looking surprised. 'We have a visitor, Davie.' Scougall was not prepared for the arrival of George Gourlay limping into the room. The brighter light of the study brought his features into sharp relief. A bald head, barrel chest, tattooed arms and neck, scars on his hands and arms. He was a daunting figure, despite his limp. A monster of a man, thought Scougall.

'You'll have a glass, Gourlay?' asked MacKenzie. Gourlay nodded. MacKenzie went to his table and filled three glasses with claret.

'I'm sorry to disturb you at home, gentlemen,' Gourlay said, sinking into an armchair opposite Scougall. 'I know a visit from a man like me may be a surprise, so I'll get straight to the point. I've heard something you might find of interest about Aeneas MacLeod.'

'Go on,' said MacKenzie, taking a seat beside Scougall.

'First, I need to ask a favour in return. I'm a businessman, after all.'

'What do you want?'

'I need a little legal work – a few documents and a couple of instruments on a property transaction.'

'I'm sure Mr Scougall will help you with it,' MacKenzie said, but Scougall was not pleased by the prospect of this work. Gourlay was hardly the kind of client he sought. But he kept his mouth shut.

'Thank you, Mr Scougall. I'll send my son to your office tomorrow morning. Now, MacLeod. He was seen with Captain Stein by my man on the night of the 20th of June, a week before the storm. I believe it was the last day he was seen alive. They were drinking together in the Ship Inn. They left at a late hour, near midnight. MacLeod appeared inebriated.'

'Why are you telling us this?' asked MacKenzie.

'I have my reasons, ones of business.'

'Are you implying Stein and MacLeod were business associates or that Stein killed MacLeod?'

'Or was it both, Mr MacKenzie?' Gourlay replied. 'I don't know all the details. I'll let you find out for yourself. But there's clearly a connection between them. Mrs Hair's writer and the Captain of the Town Guard sharing bottle after bottle? A strange duo, indeed.'

CHAPTER 23

Dewarton House

THE NEXT DAY they rode up through the Pleasance and out of the city to the south, passing Craigmillar Castle on a ridge to the left. MacKenzie looked pre-occupied and Scougall did not trouble him with questions. Scougall himself was finding it difficult to concentrate on the case. An image kept coming back to him, the image of Christina Munro. He wondered if his mother had talked to her parents already. He wondered if she wanted to see him again.

They crossed the North Esk at the bottom of Lugton Brae and stopped in Dalkeith to take some refreshments. When they had taken a table in a tavern on the Dalkeith High Street, MacKenzie handed Scougall a letter. 'This arrived last night after you left, Davie.' Scougall recognised the hand immediately. He had corresponded with her himself in the past. It was from Elizabeth. He read the short letter:

26 July 1689

My beloved father,

I'm sorry I have not written to you during the last few weeks. It was due to the dangerous circumstances I find myself in. I am in the train of the army which moves continuously through the hills. The marches have been relentless and hard. All outward mail is restricted. I managed to get this out with a messenger bound for Edinburgh. We believe we will meet the enemy soon in battle. Dundee is convinced of our victory. Let us hope for success against the foe.

I can say little just now except to tell you I love you very much and miss you with all my heart. I will explain many things to you when we see each other again. I hope, God willing, it will be soon. I will add only that a woman in my condition, during a time of war, must be very careful.

Please give my love to Meg and Archie and of course to Mr Scougall and Mr Stirling. I hope these difficult days find them all in good health.

Your beloved daughter,
Elizabeth

'It is good news, sir. She's alive!' Scougall blurted out.

'It's a relief to receive this.' MacKenzie patted Scougall warmly on the shoulder and took back the letter. 'It's still a worrying time, though. God knows what might happen if MacKay crushes Dundee's army.' MacKenzie looked down at the letter in his hand as if it was a holy relic. He was delighted with the suggestion she had written before, the other letters were probably lost, he assumed. Something else, however, had sent his spirits soaring. It was only hinted in the letter but he knew what she meant: she was with child. The thought of a grandchild vanquished the black bird completely. It became a speck and then nothing. There was so much to live for if she came back to him safely. The thought of a child at the Hawthorns again was wonderful. He imagined his grandchild playing in the gardens. He told himself he must not get carried away. He had a killer to find first.

He wanted to tell Scougall everything but he could not. He was getting ahead of himself. What if Elizabeth was already married? The child might be raised in the Highlands, or even abroad. It was likely the child would be brought up a Papist. That would be a disaster. He had nothing against the Papist religion per se, but it would deny the child a comfortable life in Scotland or anywhere else in Britain. And then a worse thought entered his mind. What if Elizabeth died in childbirth like his wife? He did not think he could survive that again. He saw the black speck in his mind again. He wished he had a God he could pray to for her safe return.

Refreshed after their break, they continued through the pleasant countryside south of Dalkeith. It was only an hour's ride to Dewarton House, an impressive edifice. MacKenzie recalled that the earl had spent a fortune on rebuilding it over the last decade, even employing Dutch artists to paint the ceilings.

A servant took care of their horses at the front gate. Another, to their surprise, frisked them for concealed weapons. They were then shown into an imposing hall with a huge staircase. The walls were crammed with portraits of the Cranstoun family. 'The Earl is hunting, gentlemen,' said the servant in an English accent. Dewarton had got rid of most of his Scottish servants for more refined ones from the south. 'He's expected back soon. Please follow me.'

They passed through corridors to the back of the house, entering a large library, full of leather-bound volumes. French doors opened onto a patio overlooking extensive gardens to the rear of the house. Scougall took in the fine view of lawns, fountains and formal boxed flowerbeds.

'It's a bonnie spot. What hills are those, sir?'

MacKenzie laughed. 'They are barely hills to a Highland man! The flat-topped Lammermuirs to the east and the Moorfoots to the west. The Vale of Tyne lies before us. You can just see the battlements of Crichton Castle through the trees.'

They sat at a table on the patio where they were served wine. For a while, they relaxed in silence, taking in the view and enjoying the warmth of the sun on their faces, resting their legs after the ride. Scougall at last summoned up courage to mention Elizabeth. 'I'm glad she's well, sir. I know it's difficult for you... but I'm glad... she's well, that she's alive, I mean,' he stammered and turned crimson.

MacKenzie put his glass down and turned to him, dropping his voice. 'I'm glad too, Davie. Thank God she's alive. We must wait and see what happens. When we know where she is, we'll be able to do something.'

Scougall could not bring himself to ask more. He had also picked up the hint in the letter of Elizabeth's pregnancy, but he felt deflated by it. A child would bind her to Ruairidh MacKenzie for ever.

In the distance from the woods, a small party of horsemen appeared. 'The Earl returns from the hunt,' said MacKenzie, pointing to the south.

The three horsemen came down the broad path through the formal gardens. When they reached the house, MacKenzie and Scougall got to their feet and bowed as Dewarton dismounted.

'John MacKenzie, your lordship, and Davie Scougall, notary public.'

Dewarton was a tall, thin, middle-aged man, with a long wig, wearing a blue velvet coat and breeches. He was dressed impeccably in the latest Paris fashions.

'Ah, Mr MacKenzie,' Dewarton said. 'My neighbour, Stirling, always speaks warmly of you. I believe you are old friends?'

'We are, my lord. We began in the Faculty of Advocates together and have been through many scrapes over the years. I heard you've been out of the country recently?'

'I've spent too much time abroad. Sadly, when I finally return to the fold, I find my King is gone. It breaks my heart. A Kingdom without a King is like a man without a wife.'

Dewarton sat at the table on the patio and indicated they should join him.

'So, what can I do for you, gentlemen?' he asked, taking off his feathered hat and placing it on the table. It was immediately removed by a servant.

'I'm engaged in a particular case, my lord. I represent the kin of Aeneas MacLeod, deceased.'

Dewarton raised his eyebrows. 'Then it's not a social call you make, MacKenzie. It's a disturbing case. He was, I hear, an accomplished young man. A great loss to his family, country and King.'

'Did you ever meet him, my lord?'

Dewarton took a deep breath. 'I knew him, although not well. He was doing some work for me. Work of a legal nature. Examining my finances, exploring how my debts might be redeemed by wadsets. The usual business of a writer. He was most accomplished in this sphere.'

'Why did you use the office of Mrs Hair?' asked MacKenzie casually. 'It was her office you used? Or did you employ him in a private capacity?'

Dewarton looked surprised when the name of Mrs Hair was mentioned. He put his glass down on the table, spilling a little wine. 'I've used her services before. She's well known as skilled in this area. I've borrowed from her in the past. I may have to borrow from her again in the future.'

'Has the business you refer to been concluded?' MacKenzie declined the offer of more wine from the servant by putting his hand over his glass.

'MacLeod made a number of recommendations to me just before he disappeared. No final decisions have been taken yet, although I think I'll follow most of them. His death has put a temporary stop to proceedings until Mrs Hair appoints another lawyer to look after it all.'

MacKenzie's tone sharpened. 'Can you think of any reason why he was killed?' He kept his gaze fixed on Dewarton's face. 'I presume you know his throat was cut and his body dumped at Craigleith?'

Dewarton finished his drink. He gave no indication of being unnerved. 'Mr MacKenzie, Mr Scougall. I'm sadly aware of the details. How can I put this… at such a sensitive time, when the new government is not secure, the new King, as some call him, fears the verdict of the people of Scotland on his seizure of the throne. I believe his government ministers make use of the dark arts. It's the foreign way of doing things. It's the Dutch way. You'll recall the assassination of William the Silent, a brutal, unlawful murder.'

'What do you mean, my lord?' asked MacKenzie.

'Let me spell it out more bluntly. Aeneas was killed because he was a supporter of the rightful king – King James.

The government wants to silence supporters of the old King. MacLeod was viewed as a danger. The government killed him. I don't know who cut his throat and dumped him in a pit, but I'm sure Dalrymple was behind it.'

'Why was MacLeod killed, my lord? Why not a more important figure among those favouring the old King?'

'He was, I think, important to the organisation of the cause. With his removal, the movement loses its effectiveness in the city. I would not be surprised if others are dispatched in a similar manner, especially if Dundee makes progress in the North or the old King has success in Ireland.'

'Who are you thinking of, your grace?'

Dewarton smiled urbanely and finished another glass. He called for more wine. 'I'm not going to admit to treason, Mr MacKenzie. I'm not going to name anyone. I don't know Mr Scougall's politics. I would guess they are not Jacobite!'

Scougall blurted out: 'I avoid taking sides at such a time, your grace... if I can!'

'A worthy position, Mr Scougall. But sometimes we cannot remain aloof.' Dewarton beckoned to another servant who ran over and began to pull off his long, black leather spurred boots.

'Who do you think carried out the killing?' asked MacKenzie.

'Many men will take a fee to kill. A Presbyterian zealot for example or a soldier returned from the wars.' The servant returned with a pair of slippers and helped Dewarton into them.

'Are you worried about your own safety, your grace?' asked MacKenzie, recalling that Stein was a soldier returned from the wars and Scobie was a Presbyterian zealot.

Dewarton quaffed another glass and stood up. He pulled back his coat to reveal a long pistol. 'Look yonder...' He pointed to the side of the garden. There was a man with a musket at the far side of the lawn and another patrolling the south wall. Dewarton pointed to the roof where another guard was stationed. 'I'm forced to set guards twenty-four hours a day. You were searched on arriving?'

'We were, most assiduously. Our country is at a dangerous juncture. There are too many men with too many weapons everywhere.'

Scougall looked around nervously. He felt cowed in Dewarton's company. He felt oppressed by the earl's air of superiority. He was just a lad from Musselburgh. He hated the arrogance of the aristocracy. He despised the way they treated their retainers and servants. He had hoped that they would be brought down a peg or two by the Revolution but one group had just replaced another. He wondered how close Dewarton and MacLeod really were.

'Is there anything else you can tell us about MacLeod?' MacKenzie could tell the earl was growing bored of their company.

'I cannot think of anything. Now, it's time I took a bath, gentlemen.'

MacKenzie made to rise, then sat back again. 'What about the... *Fidelis Homines*?'

Dewarton took a handkerchief from his pocket and blew his nose. 'Never heard of it.' MacKenzie knew there was a hint of panic in the earl's expression which he was trying to cover up. Dewarton was clearly lying.

'It's a small group of supporters of the old King. MacLeod was one and Drummond and... yourself?'

'You are mistaken, sir. I belong to no such group.' Dewarton stared back at him.

'You've never met MacLeod, Drummond and a man known as Argentum?'

Dewarton looked away to the hills in the south. The spark of anger was gone. He was tranquil again. 'I've never met them together. I don't know anyone by that name.'

MacKenzie bowed his head. He knew Dewarton was lying and Dewarton knew he knew. They did not have to say any more about it. Dewarton and MacLeod belonged to *Fidelis Homines* but Dewarton would never admit to it, that would be betraying his King. 'I'm sorry we were mistaken, sir. We've made a wasted journey to Dewarton. Now, turning to happier matters, how do your negotiations with Archibald proceed?'

Dewarton appeared to relax. He turned his eyes back on them and smiled. 'Stirling has a very fine daughter. She's beautiful and accomplished. My son is quite smitten with her. A date is set for the ceremony at last. Everything is settled. It will be a joyous day for both families. We've negotiated long and hard as good neighbours should.'

'Archibald has been much taken up with it. His health has suffered.'

Dewarton smiled sardonically. 'I believe he does not like the taste of the new regime either.'

'Another reluctant Jacobite like yourself, my lord,' suggested MacKenzie.

'No, I would not describe him as reluctant. He's as staunch a Jacobite as I know. He never tires of telling me about Montrose's miraculous victories and loyalty to the King's father.'

They thanked the Earl and took their leave retracing their steps through the house. Their horses were ready for them having been fed and watered.

As they cantered down the drive, MacKenzie had a revelation. The loyal men had surely met in Dewarton House. Bellum was war, and 'w…a…r' were three letters in the name of the house. It was only a short journey to Tyneford, a small village to the east of Dewarton House, situated at a well-worn crossing point over the Tyne Water. They rode down a long slope through woods of birch and alder. Stirling's house was on the far side of the stream. It was a fine dwelling with crow-stepped gables, a central turret and white harled walls. On the south side was a walled garden. They were shown into the library by his servant.

The room was in a state of chaos. Book cases were crammed with tomes. Towers of books rose from the floor around the desk. Papers were strewn everywhere. The overall impression was of a chamber bursting at the seams. The desk itself was piled high with volumes, so that the person sitting there to write could hide behind a wall of words.

They took a seat on a couch, on which books rested at both ends, beside a fire which had just been lit. Stirling arrived a few minutes later. He was wigless and it seemed he had lost much of his hair over the last few months. He still looked tired and drawn but was pleased to see them.

'This is a surprise, gentlemen. But a most pleasant one. A sight for sore eyes, indeed. Welcome to my humble abode, Davie. You haven't visited me here before?'

'No, sir. It's a bonnie spot.' Scougall was disconcerted by the complete chaos of Stirling's library. His nature craved order and he reflected that he would begin tidying up if he was left alone there.

'We were visiting Dewarton,' said MacKenzie. 'He told us you were home. We thought we'd pay you a visit on our way back to Edinburgh.'

Stirling looked perturbed. 'Why were you visiting him?'

'MacLeod was carrying out legal work for him.'

'I see. What kind of work?' Stirling looked unsettled and agitated.

'Dewarton's finances are a mess. Mrs Hair was having a look at them. She intended to buy some of the heavily discounted bonds. You'll no doubt be aware of this given your negotiations with him.'

Stirling sighed. 'Some wine, gentlemen?' He called for his servant to bring a bottle. 'Everything is settled now. I'm glad to say. It's a huge weight off my shoulders, John. He may have told you. In two months, I must pay the first part of the tocher. I'll be poor, but the family of Stirling will be enriched with honour.'

'When is the ceremony?' asked Scougall, trying to make conversation. He thought Stirling would have preferred if they left.

'In a few weeks. The exact arrangements are not finalised.' Stirling gave a nervous smile and finished his glass. 'I hope my life can then return to normal. I'm desperate to get back to my books. As you see, they're in a state of disorder!' He looked around and shook his head. 'How did I ever let it get into this state,' he mused.

'Did you ever see MacLeod during the negotiations at Dewarton House?' asked MacKenzie.

'No. I think he just prepared documents. I saw his name on a few of them. I knew him not, although I heard much about him.'

MacKenzie was worried about his friend's appearance but he did not want to upset him by fretting. He continued to ask questions casually. 'What about Dewarton's political position? It's said he's an active plotter like MacLeod.'

'I know only what's said about him, John. Dewarton does not confide in me about anything like that. I've heard it said he's a Jacobite. I do not doubt it.'

'He's more active than you, Archibald?'

Stirling looked uncomfortable. 'I would say so. An important lesson of the civil war is that being too eager to take a side at an early stage can prove fatal.'

'Have you heard anything more about MacLeod's death?'

Stirling began to shake his head, but stopped. He had remembered something. 'There's one thing you might be interested in. A few days ago, I was taking a bottle in town when I bumped into an old acquaintance. A man who supplied the Crown Office with information. He tried to get some money out of me when I asked him about MacLeod. But he eventually told me anyway when I said I had none. He told me MacLeod was thick with Abraham Slight, the merchant who was killed in the Canongate explosion. Slight was playing a deep game, pretending to support William, but working secretly for King James.'

'If that was the case, he was unlucky to be killed in an explosion engineered by Jacobites,' said MacKenzie, perplexed by the different visions of Slight, one from Scougall and one from Stirling.

'I don't understand, sir. Slight is known as a loyal Presbyterian,' added Scougall.

'At this time of political disruption, it's difficult to take anyone at face value, Davie,' said Stirling.

MacKenzie took out his pipe and began to fill it with tobacco. 'I spoke to Dalrymple, Archibald. It was sad to be in the Advocate's office without Rosehaugh. Dalrymple admitted MacLeod was being followed by one of his spies. He would not tell me who the man was. We have, however, learned he goes by the code name of Kyle. Does that mean anything to you?'

Stirling thought for a few moments. 'It's an area in Ayrshire. Otherwise, it means nothing more to me.'

MacKenzie puffed on his pipe, thinking. After a few moments he asked: 'Do you have Blaeu's Maps?'

Stirling went to the other side of the room and rummaged in a pile of books. He came back with a large dusty tome which he handed to MacKenzie. 'Find Mackieston Mill on the River Ayr, Davie,' said MacKenzie passing the volume to Scougall.

Scougall turned the pages to find the map of Kyle. There was a plethora of place names crammed on the map and his eyes took a while to register anything familiar. At last he found the town of Ayr. His eyes followed the River Ayr east, coming eventually to Mackieston Mill. 'I've found it, sir.'

'Anything interesting about it?' asked MacKenzie, moving closer to Scougall to look himself.

Scougall looked hard at the map but could not see anything out of the ordinary.

'Give it to me, Davie.' MacKenzie took the heavy book on his lap. He bent down close and scanned it carefully. After a couple of minutes, a smile spread across his face. 'Interesting, gentlemen. There is a village near Mackieston called Stair.' MacKenzie got to his feet and wandered over to the window. He said nothing for a while, but puffed on his pipe. He just stood there, silently, like a large stone. At last he turned and spoke: 'On another matter, Archibald. I have good news. A letter arrived from Elizabeth. She's with Dundee's army. I'm pleased, of course, but worried too.'

'Good news at last,' said Stirling. He looked genuinely pleased. 'Let's share a glass and drink to her safe return.'

CHAPTER 24

The Morning After

IN THE HOUR BEFORE dawn Gourlay's tavern continued doing a reasonably brisk trade. Late stragglers from other drinking dens sought a place where they could continue their journey into inebriation. From the inconspicuous door staggered those who had finally given up the ghost, to wander off to sleep in a dark vennel, or if lucky, a bed in a chamber. Music could still be heard inside, not the raucous fiddling of the early hours, but a restrained and melancholic sound as customers demanded breakfast to kill hangovers.

At dawn, the light was still thin. Thick clouds hung low in the sky and for an hour thereafter nobody noticed the indistinct shape at the right-hand side of the door. It was just a man smoking a last pipe before going home or urinating in the first convenient spot outside the howff. It was an hour and a half after sunrise that a servant girl, having finished her shift, came out the door and saw the shape clearly when she turned her head. Her frantic screams brought folk out of the tavern and the neighbouring tenements. A small crowd quickly gathered around a headless torso dripping with blood which was resting on a wooden frame.

'Who is it?' was the question on everyone's lips.

A man moved closer, mesmerised by the bleeding stumps where legs and arms had been cleaved from the body. There was a deep gash in the groin. The sexual organs had been cut off. The thorax was a powerful one and easily identified by markings on the chest. Only one man in the city had a tattoo of a dolphin under his right nipple. It was the owner of the establishment himself.

'Christ Almighty! It's Gourlay!' Aye, it's him!' 'The Jacobite bastards have killed George Gourlay!'

CHAPTER 25

A Ride to Stirling

MACKENZIE AND SCOUGALL returned to Mrs Hair's office the day after seeing Stirling. 'She's gone to Garlet House for a few days, gentlemen,' said Galbraith. He did not look pleased to see them again.

MacKenzie looked annoyed. 'I wanted to ask her something important.'

'She usually only stays a few days.'

'Then I have a question or two for you, Mr Galbraith.'

Galbraith looked anxious. 'I'm very busy this morning, Mr MacKenzie. I'm responsible for the office in her absence.'

'I'll only keep you a couple of minutes. We've heard that you crossed with MacLeod.'

'How do you mean, sir?'

'He said something disrespectful about your wife.'

Galbraith looked down at his feet. Scougall noticed his fists were clenched tightly. He did not meet MacKenzie's eyes. 'He was like that. Tried to get under your skin, if he noticed weakness. I don't care for jokes about Mary. What right did he have to joke about her... scum like him!'

'I didn't realise you felt so strongly about him.'

'I didn't like him, Mr MacKenzie. I don't know why she employed him here. It was like she was blind as far as he was concerned.'

'Would you say you hated him?' MacKenzie asked provocatively and waited for Galbraith's reaction.

Galbraith nodded. 'I hated him. But not enough to kill him, if that's what you're thinking. My wife is with child. Why would I risk everything? I'm a cautious man. Ask Mrs Hair. I've served her for fifteen years. Would I throw it all away because of a fool like MacLeod!'

'Come, Davie. We ride for Garlet House. We need to see Mrs Hair right away,' said MacKenzie turning on his heel. Scougall followed reluctantly. He was fed up of all this gandering about. He wanted to spend a few hours on the Links but he knew golf would have to wait until they had solved the case.

They took horses from the Cowgate, leaving the city through the West Port and heading through the fields on the Linlithgow Road. MacKenzie drove his horse on urgently and Scougall struggled to keep up. MacKenzie wanted to get there and back by sundown. On the road, Scougall's mind kept drifting back to Christina. She was a spark of life, making him laugh, lifting his spirits. She was not a beauty like Elizabeth or Agnes, but she was bonnie enough for him. MacKenzie kept his head down as they galloped along. He wanted this case finished so he could concentrate on Elizabeth again. They could not stop now. He had the feeling that an answer would come to them soon.

From Stirling, they took fresh horses for Alloa, a small town a few miles away, following the River Forth. Garlet House sat on its own, not far from the town, recognisable from the painting on Mrs Hair's office wall. It was a simple building, not grand but homely, with an orchard at one side, a walled garden to the rear and flowerbeds at the front, all framed by a fine view of the Ochil Hills. Scougall was exhausted by the ride and was relieved to dismount. He reflected how pleasant it would be to have a place in the country, a sanctuary from the city away from the world of business, a safe place to raise children. Maybe he would find somewhere near Musselburgh; invest some of his money in a home for him and Chrissy! He told himself to stop fantasising, but a picture of wedded bliss kept invading his mind.

'Follow me, Davie,' said MacKenzie as they reached the front door. 'We don't have any time for formalities!'

MacKenzie tried the door. It was unlocked. He went straight inside without knocking, Scougall following nervously behind. He was getting used to MacKenzie's dismissal of social niceties on a case but he did not like it, by nature he was a conformist. They found themselves in a small hall. The door into the sitting room on the left was ajar. They heard a muffled: 'Who is it?' MacKenzie knocked but then entered immediately. Mrs Hair was sitting at a desk writing with a quill, dressed in her usual attire. She looked up in surprise. On the couch by the window, busy with needlework was a young woman. Scougall was surprised to see it was Betty McGrain.

'Guests usually knock, Mr MacKenzie.' She did not seem displeased to see them, but MacKenzie sensed that she was caught off-guard. It was the first time he had seen her flustered. She put her quill down.

'Forgive me, madam. We're in a rush… we're in a rush. I need an answer to a particular question which is troubling me… perhaps you can help?'

'Very well, Mr MacKenzie. You've come a long way, please take a seat.' She picked up a small bell on the desk and rang it. A surprised servant was dispatched for refreshments.

MacKenzie waited for Mrs Hair to gather her composure. He was deliberately silent, waiting for her to explain. Scougall sat nervously, wondering if he should break the silence. Finally, she spoke: 'Betty isn't just a servant in the office. She's much more than that. She's my niece. I don't advertise it but she's my brother's daughter. She's his… bastard, I hate that word, but it's used by men, so I'm forced to use it… her mother was a maid in my father's house… my brother was fond of her. She died in childbirth. My brother was taken by the Lord many years ago. I took Betty under my wing. I've looked after her and overseen her education. I've trained her in the ways of business. She'll be an independent woman when I die and a wealthy one.' She became more confident as she talked.

MacKenzie was still on his feet. He moved to the desk and glowered down on Mrs Hair. 'MacLeod abused your niece, Mrs Hair, not just a servant. Did you arrange to have him killed?'

Mrs Hair smiled weakly. 'Sit down, Mr MacKenzie. Don't be so silly. Why on earth would I do something foolish like that?'

MacKenzie remained where he was. 'MacLeod was threatening your young protégé. He had even told her that you yourself would be dead soon and he would take over the office. Was he hinting that he was going to kill you? Everything you had worked for would pass to the rogue.' She shook her head dismissively. 'It is nonsense, sir!' MacKenzie retreated to sit on the couch beside Scougall. Betty remained where she was, silently observing them.

'I could have found other ways to deal with him,' said Mrs Hair adamantly. 'I could have ended his employment. I could have asked him to travel to Jamaica on a trading voyage where it's likely he would have succumbed to one of the diseases prevalent there. But murder him! Besides everything, it's morally wrong. It would be acting like him, like a pathetic, arrogant man.'

'Can you prove you did not arrange his killing?' MacKenzie was impressed by her self-control.

'Do you have any evidence, Mr MacKenzie?' She took off her glasses and placed them on the desk.

'We have a witness who saw Betty threatening him with a knife and heard her say she wanted him dead. She told us herself she was pleased by his death. It's obvious he behaved disgracefully towards her. In some circles, it might be said he deserved to die. He treated her atrociously. Did Betty kill him in a fit of anger? Were you forced to tidy things up? Pay someone to bury the body?' MacKenzie turned to Betty. She had put down her needlework. 'I ask you again, Betty. Did you kill Aeneas MacLeod?'

She said nothing. But tears were on her cheeks.

'This is fanciful nonsense, Mr MacKenzie,' continued Mrs Hair. 'I'll tell you why Betty cannot be responsible. She was seriously ill at the time. She was confined to bed when MacLeod disappeared. She was in no state to do anything.'

'Can you prove it, madam?'

'Ask the doctor who treated her – Adam Lawtie.' MacKenzie sighed inwardly at the mention of his name.

'We'll check with him, madam, to verify what you say. What of your associates, the men who would kill for money... men like Gourlay and Stein?'

'They are not my associates, Mr MacKenzie. I've done some business with Gourlay over the years. I know he's a rogue. As for Stein, I've never had anything to do with him. I've never even spoken to him.'

'Why did you employ MacLeod, madam? He has caused nothing but trouble in your office. He has upset Betty, Galbraith, Scobie and no doubt others. Was he worth it?'

Mrs Hair's tone sharpened. She would only put up with so much under her own roof. She knew MacKenzie was on the trail of a killer but enough was enough. 'I'll tell you why I employed him, Mr MacKenzie. He knew the Highlands. He knew about land there. He recommended I should buy certain bonds. I bought at five pence in the pound and sold a few months later at two shillings in the pound. I made a lot of money from Aeneas MacLeod. I made thousands of pounds. And in that he served me well, gentlemen. But I am sorry he caused so much... devastation in the office.'

MacKenzie rose abruptly and he let himself relax. 'We are sorry for interrupting your leisure. We will take our leave immediately,' he said affably. 'Come, Davie. We must get back to Edinburgh right away.' He was pleased with himself. They had established the true relationship between Betty and Mrs Hair and he felt convinced they were not involved in MacLeod's killing. However, they would check with Lawtie about Betty's health.

CHAPTER 26

News from the North

IT WAS ALMOST dark when they finally got back to the city exhausted after the long ride. They were surprised to find the whole place in a state of complete uproar bordering on pandemonium. The streets were still packed with people despite the late hour. Men, women and children everywhere, shouting and screaming. Scougall was reminded of the days of the Revolution the previous year and his heart sank.

They dismounted their horses and stood watching the scene, perplexed. MacKenzie stopped a man on the street and asked what had happened.

'News from the north, sir. Terrible news! The armies clashed near Blair. Dundee was victorious! The Jacobites defeated MacKay! MacKay's army was routed. Dundee marches south to take the Lowlands!'

Scougall was dumbfounded. There had been no doubt in his mind that Dundee would be crushed. 'My God, how can it be!'

'A Highland army should never be written-off, Davie.' MacKenzie was also surprised but he was not devastated like Scougall. His first thought was for Elizabeth. It was good news for her. It should hopefully mean she was safe. But the aftermath of a battle was very dangerous, even for those in the train of the victorious side.

Everyone on the streets was hungry for news. It was immediately obvious that the Jacobites in the city were becoming more vocal. They now felt secure enough to come out into the open and, on every corner, intoxicated by the stupendous news, they were drunkenly toasting King James.

Scougall and MacKenzie stood outside the Tron Kirk on the High Street observing the mayhem. Scougall was appalled by the sudden confidence of the Jacobites. 'Come, Davie. Let's use this opportunity to our advantage,' said MacKenzie, taking his arm. Scougall did not understand what he meant but followed him up the High Street. MacKenzie stopped at the corner of a vennel opposite the Tollbooth. 'Keep an eye on the door,' he said, indicating the main entrance in front of them.

They loitered. They watched. It grew darker. The crowds did not disperse. It was now dark. The city was still in uproar. A mob of government supporters had coalesced in the Lawnmarket. They marched up and down noisily chanting how they would cull the Jacobites. Groups of supporters of the old King were meeting down vennels and closes. There was going to be trouble.

The Tollbooth door eventually opened. Stein was at the front of his guards. They were heavily armed, expecting unrest on the streets.

'Quick, Davie! Now's our chance.' MacKenzie wanted to use the opportunity to slip inside the Tollbooth unseen. He was looking for evidence linking MacLeod with Stein. They waited for the last guard to disappear into the crowd. MacKenzie crossed the street with Scougall following. They were in luck. The door was not locked. As they entered, a guard who had remained behind disappeared around the corner at the bottom of the corridor. MacKenzie whispered that he was probably going to keep an eye on the prisoners. He opened the door of the guard's quarters on the left. There was no one in the room. The door to Stein's chamber was shut. MacKenzie tried the handle. It was locked. He looked around for something to use. An old sword lay against the wall in a corner. He began to lever open the door, while Scougall nervously kept watch at the other door. Stein's door gave way after a few tries. Scougall closed the outer door and they entered Stein's office. Scougall lit a candle from a torch on the wall, and MacKenzie closed the door behind them and took another candle himself.

'If Stein comes back we'll have a bit of explaining to do, sir!' whispered Scougall, fearfully.

'The nonsense on the streets will keep them busy all night, Davie, I'm sure of it.'

They began to search the room. Scougall examined the piles of weapons while MacKenzie looked in the desk. The drawers were locked. He took a small metal tool from his cloak and forced one open, rummaging through it hastily. It was full of coins, notes, account books, letters. He rifled them quickly. The papers were written in many different hands and the account books were of different sizes, mostly itemising the purchase and sale of weapons. He forced the other drawer. More papers. Then, something caught his eye – the handwriting on a small account book. It was a hand he recognised.

'Look, Davie! MacLeod's memorandum book!'

Scougall held up the candle to make it easier to read. MacKenzie scanned the pages quickly.

'What's it doing here? Do you think Stein killed MacLeod?' asked Scougall earnestly.

'This is not direct evidence of that. But how did Stein get it? He must be involved in some way.'

MacKenzie handed Scougall the book which he put in his pouch. Suddenly, there was a noise outside in the guard room. Had the remaining guard returned? He might notice the door had been forced. Scougall froze. MacKenzie's eyes darted round the room. Stirling had mentioned to him years ago there was a way down into the cellars from the chamber. An old rug lay on the floor behind the desk. He pulled it back. There was a trapdoor underneath. He yanked at the small metal handle. It wouldn't come up so he dashed back to the drawers where he had seen a bunch of keys stored in one of them. As quietly as he could, he tried each key in the trapdoor lock. The third worked. He heaved up the door. He looked down and saw stone steps, worn by age, descending into the darkness.

'Are we going in there?' asked Scougall in a whisper, disgust on his face.

'We've no choice, Davie, until we can get out.'

They each took a candle and descended. Scougall closed the trapdoor above. They went down, down, down into pitch darkness. Scougall counted twenty, thirty steps until they reached flat ground. He held up his candle. They were in a large vaulted room. A wooden chair stood alone in the middle. A few metal implements lay in the shadows in a corner. They went over to examine them, Scougall holding up the candle. He was not sure at first what he was looking at. MacKenzie picked something up and held it beside the candle. It was a metal contraption of some kind. 'A thumbscrew, Davie!' Then the grisly collection around them came into focus: thumbscrews, daggers and swords of different shapes and sizes. Against the wall was a long pole with a huge blade at the top. Scougall held up the candle. 'A halberd, sir.'

They could see an opening at the far side of the room and moved down a narrow corridor slowly. Rats scurried in the darkness. Walls dripped onto the mud floor. They found themselves in another chamber. The smell of decay was overpowering. An object hung in the darkness from the ceiling. They moved slowly to get a closer look. Scougall winced. MacKenzie turned away. It was parts of a human body, butchered and flailed, oozing white maggots. 'Who is he?'

'I don't know, Davie. The carter from the quarry perhaps – Rab Christie? This is Stein's torture chamber.'

'If he catches us, sir!' Scougall nodded at the shape in the darkness.

'There are ways out of this labyrinth. Stirling told me about theses cellars. They were built hundreds of years ago. There are ways out. We just need to find one!'

They moved cautiously down another corridor into a longer room. Wooden boxes covered the floor. MacKenzie opened one and saw a selection of pistols lying on straw. In another long box were swords.

Scougall began to feel nauseous. His mind flashed back to his incarceration the previous year with the Harlequin. He imagined they had descended into Hell. The Devil was seeking them out. He could be round the next corner. Yet he said nothing to MacKenzie – he wanted, above all, to prove himself to him. He was not just a feeble clerk.

They plodded on through the darkness, down passageway after passageway, through room after room. They were all empty except for scurrying rats in their hundreds. They passed on an on, under the city, through another city. God knew to where! How long had they been down there? Ten minutes, twenty, thirty?

Suddenly, somewhere, there was a sound. It was impossible to tell if it came from the next room or a mile away. Was it the sound of the trapdoor being heaved open? The guard had noticed the rug was moved. Was Stein returning for them? Scougall's blood froze; his heart thudded with fear. They quickened their pace. On and on they went into the labyrinth. It felt like they were hopelessly lost. Scougall followed MacKenzie, silently, concentrating on his boots.

There were more sounds in the darkness. Was it men following them or just the rats that swarmed everywhere in profusion. The image of the body hanging like a flesher's carcass at the forefront of their thoughts. They heard another sound, this time closer. They both stopped and looked back. There was a moment's flash of light in the distance, down the long corridor behind them. Was it Stein himself who was on their trail or another guard? They both feared the worst. The light was gone in a second. Had he taken another route? He would surely know the chambers like the palm of his hand. Was he going to cut them off? Would they be surrounded?

'Quick, Davie. We have to keep going.'

Scougall's mind imagined Stein on their tracks, getting closer by the second. He would have no hesitation in killing them. But he would want to extract information first. They had no excuses for being there. They would surely be tortured. He focused on the movement of his body, following MacKenzie through the blackness. He began to pray. God deliver us. God deliver us. God deliver us.

MacKenzie was worried. He had hoped to find a way out before now. He feared they were going round in a circle. Had he taken them into a trap? He was annoyed at himself. They should have waited, been more cautious. He didn't want to die down here, just as Elizabeth was returned to him. He felt anger rising in his soul. He must fight on for her and his grandchild.

They turned a sharp corner. The passageway narrowed and the ceiling was lower. There was something different at the end of it and it was not as dark. There was a small lozenge of light in the distance. They followed it down the passageway, splashing through water as they ran. There was more and more water on the floor and the ground was muddy. They slipped their way forwards and saw a small wooden door at the end of the passageway, only about four feet high, with light behind it. Moonlight. Scougall tried the handle. It was locked! He looked at MacKenzie in panic. MacKenzie held up the keys. 'Let's pray to your God, Davie.'

Scougall closed his eyes and beseeched the Lord to help them. The fourth key worked. They pulled the door open and spilled out into the fresh night air. The moon shone brightly above the trees. They had been lucky. A few minutes later they might not have found the door in the darkness. Scougall shut it and MacKenzie locked it. 'Did he see us?' asked Scougall.

'He'll not know for certain who it was. Just two shapes in the darkness.'

Scougall leaned against the bank, gathering his breath. It felt like they had been walking for miles. 'Where are we, sir?'

MacKenzie admitted he had no idea. He judged they had only been beneath the city for about thirty minutes. They could not be far away. They moved forward a few yards and faced a steep drop. There was water beneath; the sound of a river. 'The Water of Leith, Davie. We've not come too far.'

There was a sudden sound of movement behind the door, a fumbling at the lock. Was it Stein? As fast as they could, they slipped into the darkness.

CHAPTER 27

City of Fear

SCOUGALL LOOKED DOWN from his window in Mrs Baird's lodgings onto the High Street. Despite the early hour of the morning, there were armed men and soldiers roaming up and down. A canon was being dragged by a team of horses up to the castle. Some were leaving the city with their possessions packed in carts or on the backs of horses and ponies, heading for friends and relatives in the country. Others were preparing the city's defences for an attack by Dundee. The city walls were being repaired, ditches dug outside the walls, defences inspected by the councillors. Fear was in the air, intensified by the news of Gourlay's killing. Suspected Jacobites had been taken into custody in the castle. Scougall had heard that David Drummond was one of them. King William was decried in taverns and coffee houses. Pamphlets circulated describing the slaughter of MacKay's useless army, putting the fear of God into supporters of the Revolution. The Presbyterians were particularly fearful. A Jacobite army would show them no mercy. Gourlay was just the start of the slaughter.

Scougall was anxious. He imagined the slaughter of MacKay's troops in the Highlands. A description of the rout was in the morning's *Gazette*. He pictured the marauding Highland Army descending on the Lowlands, just as Montrose had taken his Papist Irish south forty years before. It was a grim prospect, the prospect of carnage. What would happen if Edinburgh fell to Dundee? Montrose's troops had raped and pillaged in Aberdeen for days. If James was re-established on the throne, MacKenzie and Stirling might be reappointed to their old positions as Clerk of the Session and Crown Officer. But what would happen to him? At least he had not been involved in politics in recent months. He was, however, known to favour Presbytery over Bishop. It was all an awful mess. Why was he born at a time of such bitter division? Could Christians not come together peaceably to solve their differences? And there was also another nagging fear. Had Stein, if it had been him in the tunnels below the city, recognised them?

Scougall was also worried about Elizabeth. Was she riding south at that very moment with her arrogant husband? Might Ruairidh return to the Hawthorns at the head of the King's soldiers? Groaning aloud, he turned from the window and slumped on his bed. Dropping his head, he put his hands together and began to pray, earnestly: 'Please preserve her, oh Lord. Please return her safely to her father. Take me instead, oh Lord.' He opened his Bible which sat on the small table beside his bed and read some passages randomly. The words had a calming effect on him. God would look after them. Trust in God. His mind drifted back to the case.

A message arrived from MacKenzie. He was to meet him outside the Tron Kirk immediately. Scougall was glad to get out of the confinement of his room and left to meet him at once. They walked down to Gourlay's howff together. MacKenzie said nothing the whole way, a cold look of determination on his face. Outside Gourlay's, Scougall was surprised to see him take a pistol from his cloak. MacKenzie did not usually carry one.

'Quick, Davie! Keep close behind me.'

Gourlay's dismembered corpse had had been removed, but bloodstains were visible on the stones around the door. They entered the howff and walked down a dark corridor which led deep into the establishment. The place was still busy despite the killing of its patron. They passed through another chamber and descended a couple of steps into a private snug. MacKenzie hid the pistol under his cloak. There was a man sitting alone at the small table. Scougall was shocked to see it was Adam Scobie who looked up in surprise. 'Excuse me, gentlemen. I'm here to see a friend.'

'Close the awning, Davie,' ordered MacKenzie calmly.

Scougall pulled the dirty curtain across the entrance. 'I'm meeting a friend here, gentlemen. You must excuse me,' said Scobie.

'You're meeting Mr Jabb, I believe,' said MacKenzie, standing in the way.

'I am, sir. How did you know? He'll be here shortly. If you could please leave me.'

'I sent the note requesting a meeting here, Mr Scobie. I addressed it to Kyle,' said MacKenzie taking out his pistol and placing it on Scobie's chest. Scougall was confused about what was happening, MacKenzie had kept him in the dark, but he moved down into the snug and stood in the corner. He felt himself begin to sweat. He remembered there was a dirk in his pocket in case he needed it. 'Search him, Davie!'

Scougall reluctantly moved towards Scobie. 'Stand!' barked MacKenzie.

Scobie raised himself slowly and held up his arms. Scougall searched him. There was a knife in his pocket and a pistol hanging from his belt. Scougall put them on the table out of reach. He frisked him again to make sure there was nothing else.

'You were ordered to follow Aeneas MacLeod by Dalrymple,' suggested MacKenzie.

Scobie said nothing.

'You're known as Kyle. You're one of Dalrymple's spies. I have it from your master.'

Scobie sat back down. 'I had no choice, sir. It's the only way I could earn a living. Please put your pistol down.'

MacKenzie did not flinch. The pistol remained pointed at Scobie's chest.

'All suspected Jacobite leaders are being watched,' continued Scobie, anxiously. 'I hold nothing against you, Mr MacKenzie. I know you're not one of the Loyal Gentlemen. But you are close to Stirling and you know Drummond and there's also your chief Seaforth. There are many other MacKenzies who are enemies of King William. Dalrymple wanted to make sure you were not a threat. I assure you you've now been taken off the list.'

'I have no involvement with Jacobites, Mr Scobie. As you well know, I'm working for a client. I'm only interested in the fate of Aeneas MacLeod.'

'You would not use that on me here surely, sir.'

MacKenzie cocked the weapon and smiled. 'You're right. I probably would not. But it might go off accidentally. It would not kill you, of course. But it might hit your leg.' He pointed the gun down at Scobie's black leather boot. 'It would be very painful. It might curtail your spying activity for a while. You'd be forced to live off your earnings from the law. I judge they are not great. I do not want to know about the Jacobite group. I don't care about the politics of it.'

'I'm not privy to Dalrymple's policies,' replied Scobie defensively. 'I only provide information for the government. I write reports for him. Dalrymple determines the policy. He decides if suspects are to be imprisoned or…'

MacKenzie waited for Scobie to finish the sentence but he did not. 'Imprisoned or what?' he asked.

'Or… extirpated,' said Scobie in a whisper.

'All I want to know is what happened to MacLeod? Was he extirpated on the orders of Dalrymple?'

'No. I don't believe so. Look, if I tell you what I know, will our conversation remain secret? Dalrymple does not need to know we've spoken. After all, MacLeod is no longer a threat. I'll tell you what I know about him.'

MacKenzie's tone shifted. He spoke calmly. 'I'm no friend of Dalrymple, Mr Scobie. What you tell us will not find its way back to him.'

Scobie slumped back and MacKenzie sat beside him but kept the pistol pointed at his leg.

'Dalrymple sought me out after I left Mrs Hair's office. The position was secured for me by relatives, Dalrymple's tenants in the west. I was on MacLeod's trail for weeks. I noted all his meetings in the city and at houses in the country. He gave me a merry dance all over the Lothians. One night, about a week before the storm at around midnight I saw MacLeod enter the Tollbooth with Stein.'

'Was he taken by force?'

'Stein and one of his men. MacLeod was drunk. They attacked him in a wynd. They beat him unconscious and dragged him inside.'

'What happened next, Mr Scobie?'

'He didn't come out again. He didn't come out again... alive.'

'Stein killed him?'

'I don't know if Stein did it himself or one of his men. I know it happened in the Tollbooth during the night. I have no evidence of the actual act. I witnessed MacLeod's entrance and exit. I've no doubt in my mind about what happened to him. I stood watching for hours in the chill night. At about four in the morning, a cart came to the side door of the Tollbooth. A heavy object was carried out by a couple of guards and dumped in the back. The men joined the carter at the front. I followed them out of the city and on to Craigleith. From cover in the woods, I watched them dig a hole and dump a body in it. They then made their way back to the city. I returned to the Tollbooth. I found bloodstains on the cobbles outside the door. The body must have been dripping blood. Since that night there was no sign of MacLeod until his body was found.'

'Stein killed MacLeod,' said Scougall from the corner.

'Yes. Stein is the killer, Davie. I believe Stein killed MacLeod and then the carter Christie to cover his tracks. But who was pulling the strings? Who ordered Stein to kill MacLeod?'

'I don't know that, gentlemen,' said Scobie, defensively. 'You must believe me when I say it.'

'Was it on Dalrymple's orders, Scobie?' asked MacKenzie, moving the pistol closer to Scobie's leg. Scougall hoped to God that MacKenzie would not use the gun on him, even if he was a spy.

'As I said already, I'm not privy to government policy. I write reports and deliver them to Dalrymple. He knew MacLeod was important in Jacobite circles,' replied Scobie earnestly.

MacKenzie put the gun down on the table and turned to Scougall: 'Who was it, Davie? Who gave the order to kill

MacLeod? Was it Dalrymple for political reasons or Mrs Hair because of his assault on Betty? Was it Drummond or Dewarton because of Jacobite rivalries? Or did Stein kill him for his own reasons?'

Scougall's mind was filled with possibilities but he had to admit to himself that he had no idea.

CHAPTER 28

Latin Nouns

IN THE EVENING they returned to Libberton's Wynd to share a nightcap. MacKenzie wanted to think. Whisky usually facilitated a fluid mind; whisky and the flames of a fire. Scougall sipped his glass slowly. He had not yet acquired a taste for the water of life. He was glad to be in MacKenzie's study rather than alone in his lodgings. He feared that Stein would be on their trail. MacKenzie finished his glass and stared into the fire, enjoying the burning sensation in his gullet. Sometimes the solution came to him in a flash, like a sudden revelation. Other times it coalesced in his mind slowly from disparate elements and was finally as clear as day and he wondered how on earth he had been so stupid. His mind buzzed with images from the previous days.

He saw it suddenly as he stared into the flames. He could hardly believe the truth. He had been stupid. He had been blind. They had been misled by one Latin word. The word was *vallum*. But the word was not *vallum* rather *vadum* instead. The two 'l's were in fact a 'd'. MacLeod's hand, described as exact by everyone, had misled them. The other meeting place was not a rampart but a shallow piece of water in a river, a ford.

MacKenzie groaned aloud, so that Scougall looked across at him worriedly. The truth was painful. He had let his prejudices blind him. He did not want to believe it. He put his empty glass down and turned to Scougall. 'The answer has been staring us in the face, Davie!'

Before MacKenzie could say anything else, Scougall blurted out: 'It must be Dalrymple, sir! He wanted rid of him as an important Jacobite... or was it Mrs Hair because of his treatment of Betty... or was Drummond vying for leadership among the Jacobites... or was Scobie lying to us?'

'Hear me out, Davie. What I have to say will be a shock.' MacKenzie's face darkened.

Scougall put his glass down and moved forward in the chair, looking baffled.

'One word has provided a solution, Davie. Once I understood it, everything slipped into place like the pieces of a jigsaw. Sadly, the face on the jigsaw is of a man we know only too well. The meeting place on the Latin list was not *vallum* but *vadum*.'

'A ford, sir,' said Scougall, still confused.

'Argentum... silver... sterling silver... vallum/vadum... rampart/ford... Tyneford House ...the other name on the list is our old friend... our friend Archibald Stirling! The initials AS are his! I think he was being blackmailed by MacLeod.'

Scougall's mouth dropped open. He could not believe it. Stirling was an honourable man and a gentleman. 'You're surely mistaken, sir. Stirling was the Crown Officer.'

'I know, Davie. It's hard to accept. Let me explain. Archibald was a key figure in Jacobite circles although he denied it. Dewarton told us as much. Archibald twice denied to me he had ever met MacLeod. He was lying. He met with the group, which included MacLeod, at the Periwig, Dewarton House and Tyneford House. The list of payments of £100 was by AS, Archibald Stirling – not Andrew Stein, Abraham Slight or Adam Scobie.'

Scougall was gravely disturbed by the interpretation. 'But why would he use Stein to kill MacLeod? Did he desire the leadership of the Jacobites himself? It's unbelievable, sir.'

MacKenzie rose from his chair. 'I don't know, Davie. But I intend to find out tonight! Take your hat!'

They marched down the High Street in darkness and climbed the stairs to Stirling's apartments in Andrew Lang's Land. MacKenzie knocked on the door but no servant answered. They waited a few moments, then tried it. It was not locked. They took a first right into Stirling's study. It was a long room full of bookcases where Stirling worked on his History when he was in town. All appeared quiet. But MacKenzie detected an unusual smell.

Scougall also noticed it. 'What's that, sir?'

MacKenzie grimaced. 'It smells like powder, Davie.'

Scougall noticed something lying on the floor behind the desk. He moved closer. MacKenzie did not follow. He was frozen to the spot by the door. Scougall looked down at a body. A pistol lay beside it on the floor.

MacKenzie was used to death but did not want to look at his dead friend. 'I cannot, Davie.'

Scougall took a few more paces forwards. He looked down on the body. Stirling's head was split open like a pomegranate. His motionless eyes stared up at the ceiling. There was a huge bullet hole in his temples. Brain matter was smeared over the wall. Scougall turned away and retched. MacKenzie cried out in despair. Memories of his friend flooded his mind. He had failed him.

Scougall pointed at the desk that was uncharacteristically tidy. Stirling had taken care to tidy it. There were two items on it. A thick manuscript titled *A History of the Rebellion* and a letter addressed to John MacKenzie, advocate.

My dear John,

I do not know if we will ever meet again. As you know I am something of a deist in religious matters and full of uncertainty about the possibility of an afterlife. We have joked many times that the first of us to die should return to visit the other from beyond the grave to enlighten him about the nature of the place, if there be one, what it is like, and so forth, so it is possible we might be re-joined, although I think we both know it unlikely.

Before I explain my recent actions, which I know will shock you, allow me a short digression into my own personal history. It may go some way to explaining what has happened. I believe I have acted during all the events I will describe as a moral agent, indeed a good Christian one, only driven to a desperate course when I could see no way out. I have only acted in this way to preserve the reputation of my beloved wife and daughter and my own as a gentleman and man of honour.

You know well I have not been entirely devoted to the public life, both during my time as an advocate and as Crown Officer. When I began my career in the law, I was always looking back fondly, too fondly, to my sojourns on the Continent when I was free to follow the whims of my nature, which directed me towards pleasure, rather than study, and which we shared, most memorably in our visit to Venice in the year 1656 when we spent a few months there together. It was a blissful summer. I enjoyed all that was good in life and that time holds its place in my memory as the happiest in my life.

A hatred of the law was imbedded in my nature from the start. The law was always grey to me, there was nothing I could do to imbue it with colour. It scunnered me and I only gradually accepted it as I matured and my ardour for a different life faded.

As you well know, I trained as an advocate because I could think of nothing else I might do to sustain my standing in society. The rising of the Session was always a great relief to me, when I could escape the city; the bucolic life allowing me time for more enjoyable pursuits including, my dear friend, the many hours of leisure spent in your convivial company, both in town and at the beautiful Hawthorns, on which I modelled my own humble estate. I have always regarded you as a noble and honest man. I wish I had followed your example in life. I know you have suffered greatly by the loss of your wife and recently your beloved daughter. I dearly hope she is returned to you as soon as fortune allows. I know you have suffered from melancholy over the years. I hope I was an amiable companion through this vale of tears we call life which we do not choose for ourselves. I have been struck by similar despondency over the years, but the afflictions I have recently suffered have been the greatest ordeal in my life. You have humoured me often when I discussed Montrose and how this realm collapsed into civil war. I know it was not always a popular subject of conversation, but if you will allow me to say it one last time, I saw much of Montrose's character in your own devotion to justice and the application of reason to human affairs during an age of distraction, an age cursed by fanatics hot for religion, in which we live. I am honoured to have called you friend.

My dear John, you will recall my initial consternation when I was offered the position of Crown Officer many years ago and your wise advice, encouraging me to take it. I must own that despite my lethargic nature I came to enjoy the work much more than I ever did pleading in the Session. It allowed me to build up a landed estate which I am very thankful for.

During the last few years, however, I have been slipping under water, and deeper and deeper have I sunk. I kept this from you. The cause of my misfortune was simple. It was occasioned by taking on too much debt and spending too much money. Since the Revolution, I have found myself drowning. My financial embarrassment escalated beyond repair, until it overwhelmed me and swept me off to sea with no sight of land. I have never followed your sound advice of being neither a lender or a borrower. I have never cut my cloth to meet the financial circumstances in which I found myself. I have been always a great spender during the whole of my life. I have loved spending on all manner of things. I have spent liberally on beautiful things which improve life: paintings, dresses for my wife and daughter, books from all corners of the world, fine furniture, numerous visits to London and the cities of Europe, a coach and horses when a mare would have done and multiplicity of servants in my household which was a vanity. I have always responded to the whims of my bedfellow and daughter by agreeing to their requests despite being short of money. As a result of my profligacy, I have built up debts well beyond a reasonable amount, indeed far beyond. It is a terrible sum, which I now believe amounts to more than ten thousand pounds sterling. I kept many of the transactions secret from you. As I was employed as Crown Officer, there was always enough money coming in to service my creditors and keep my head above water. I thought I would trim my spending as I grew older, but then everything changed.

You know something of this embarrassment, but not the whole story. In the first place, it was brought to my attention that Dewarton's youngest son had an eye for my daughter. To secure the match, which was a very good one for her, I had to borrow substantially to provide the tocher demanded by the earl and his brood of lawyers. I should have declined the match. I should have secured a less attractive candidate, but I could not break Arabella's heart and my own vanity desired it. I was forced to write bonds at high rates to secure the funding. It was at this point I borrowed from you, my loyal friend, the sum of one thousand pounds sterling, which I return to you now. The money can be found in a bag in the drawer in my desk. It was only a small part of the funds I was forced to raise by bond and by mortgaging parts of my estate.

Secondly, and more acutely, was my sudden fall from office, occasioned by recent political upheavals, which none of us could have predicted, even a year ago. This was a disaster for me. It cut off a supply of money at once which was not replaced by rents. My lands had suffered a decline in recent years by poor management. In other words, my income fell substantially, just as my outgoings increased hugely.

I apologise for this long digression. I now turn to the matter at hand. You will know I denied knowing MacLeod during our conversations over the last week or so. The rogue whose death you have been investigating was sadly only too well known to me. I am truly sorry I lied to you, my dearest friend. I hated myself for misleading you. It was a true mark of how far I had fallen from the honourable position which I believe dictated my conduct during most of my life. MacLeod belonged to a small circle of gentlemen of a Jacobite persuasion, some of whom are well known to you, including Drummond and Dewarton. I was a member of this group. We met in the country and in town at both Dewarton House and in my own house at Tyneford and sometimes in the Periwig. At first, I thought MacLeod a fine fellow hungry to fight for his King and willing to give up everything for the cause. Indeed, I thought we had become bosom friends. We entertained each other in various hostelries and got on like a house on fire. He even listened to my tales of Montrose, particularly his dealings with the clan MacLeod. However, his true nature was revealed to me one night in a tavern when I received as grave a shock as I have experienced in my whole life. After we had drunk long from the bottle, and toasted the true King many times to great cheers in the establishment, MacLeod turned to me and said, casually, he was well acquainted with my daughter. He had never mentioned this to me before, so I was taken aback. I nodded absently and knocked back another glass of claret, little expecting what would follow. He said she was a sonsie lass. I was a bit annoyed by this statement and put down my glass. He then said he would not mind taking a roll with her himself, if he got the chance. I was angered by his impertinence, particularly the lascivious way he said it. Before I had a chance to reprimand him, he declared he had heard certain stories about her which he began to describe in lurid detail, about various men who had known the pleasure of her body and other vile lies. You may know John, I was shocked to my core and disgusted by the fellow. In an instant, my anger flared up and I had him up against the wall by the neck, throttling the life out of him. I would have run him through with my sword, if I had not been stopped by the other gentlemen in the tavern. They had not heard our discussion and thought I was taken by a fit of drunken madness. We were pulled apart and I was persuaded to return to my chambers for the night. The next morning, when I awoke and remembered what had occurred, my raging anger returned. I sat in my chambers nursing a hangover and planning how I might have my revenge on him. I was surprised in the afternoon to receive a visit from him. I thought he had come to apologise for what he had said the night before and beg for my forgiveness, to admit he was a foolish fellow transported by drink. I was ready to challenge him to a duel if he did not. But what he had to say shocked me further. He sat casually in the chair opposite me and handed me a document with a smirk on his face. It was a description in writing of what he had described in the tavern the night before which alleged a number of well-known blades in the city had carnal knowledge of my daughter. He told me bluntly that if I did not pay him £100 sterling by a certain date, he would send the account to Dewarton. At first, I laughed off the attempt at blackmail, telling him it was all a pack of lies. Then he told me he had witnesses willing to testify they had seen her in the company of Colonel Charteris, a well-known rake and libertine, who frequented gambling dens in the city and who I had run into now and again myself, which sent me into a panic. I was not sure what to do. At length, to cut a long story short, after much deliberation and soul-searching, I decided to make the payment to preserve my daughter's honour. On the appointed day, I handed over the sum, hoping it would put an end to the matter. I never heard anything from him for a few weeks. I was much relieved and felt much better in myself. I continued with the marriage negotiations with Dewarton. I felt my health return and my vigour for life. I hoped the matter was over. But, of course, it was not. How could I have been so stupid? MacLeod appeared at my door again and made another request for £100. After I had paid it, he made another. I will not go into the details of these dark months when my health suffered and my soul was tortured. I drank deeply from the bottle. At times, I fell into a kind of manic frenzy. I dearly wish I had sought your council and shared the burden of my secrets with you. However, I was not in my right mind. Finally, after I had made a series of payments he demanded a retainer of fifty pounds sterling every month in perpetuity. You can well imagine how angry I was and how I cursed this spiteful creature who I would be joined to forever. He even said he would take my daughter off my hands and marry her himself if no-one would have her, she now being a piece of damaged goods. My anger smouldered like a volcano ready to burst forth. I was overcome by wild fantasies of revenge. You must understand me John, I had become desperate. My mind was in a state of frenzy akin to madness. I had to borrow more to make these payments to MacLeod and my finances were spiralling dangerously out of control. Everything was slipping away from me. If he sent the paper to Dewarton, the marriage would be called off. All my efforts would have been for nothing and I would still be heavily in debt. My wife Margaret knew nothing of all this. She was entirely taken up with arrangements for the wedding and spending large sums of money which I did not have. I bore it all on my own shoulders, although on a couple of occasions I almost unburdened myself to you on the golf course. It might have been my salvation. We will never know.

Anyway, I was grown desperate beyond belief. One night after a couple of bottles of wine, I reflected on the example of my beloved Montrose, trying to work out what he would have done in the same situation. I realised he would have acted rather than being dictated to by others. I decided I had to act myself. I had been weak. I had let events overwhelm me. I must gain the initiative. I was not without useful connections. The Town Guard were mostly a shamble of fools, but one or two of their number were skilled soldiers who had seen action in Flanders and other bloody theatres of war. Such was the example of Captain Andrew Stein. Rumours circulated about him, which I ignored when in office. He proved one of the few guards who were of any use to me. I had heard he could be bought and I was willing to pay. I believed the sum of £100 sterling which MacLeod had demanded would suffice. I was proved correct. Stein and I went for a walk outside the city walls, where after much procrastination, I proposed the transaction to him. He took half the money there and then without hesitation. He said the deed would be done in the following days. I told him the body must never be found. He assured me it would not.

There you have it, John. I have made my confession. I asked for no more details from Stein and he gave none. He would receive the other half of the money when he provided evidence of MacLeod's demise. We met again two days later. He told me it was done, showing me MacLeod's glove with his name embroidered on it. I was overjoyed when I heard of this man's death by murder, completely forgetting the Lord's Commandment. I felt a great weight lift from my shoulders. Sometimes it is right to kill, John. In this case, I believe I had natural justice on my side. I removed from the world a man who would only do ill to others during his life. I am sorry to say I had no thought for his father, foster father or clan. You can imagine my shock a week later when I read in the *Gazette* that a storm had uncovered a body near Craigleith. I did not know where Stein had disposed of MacLeod. I hoped it was just an old skeleton buried long ago. But I had nagging doubts. I began to think God wanted to punish me. I prayed that nothing would come of it. I hoped the government were too busy with the political situation and if it was MacLeod, he would be whisked off to the Highlands for burial. Then I heard you were asked to investigate the killing by MacLeod's family. I was stung to the core. I knew the methodical way you would investigate. I thought about telling you everything the night of the explosion, after we had played golf, but I could not. I am ashamed to admit I lied to you, denying I had any knowledge of MacLeod and fabricating a story about Abraham Slight to put you off the trail. I felt sometimes I was in the clear. Evidence was sparse. At such times, my spirits soared. I felt like my old self again. I looked positively to the future. So much else was happening in town that a writer's killing would not interest anyone. I prayed my ordeal was over.

But I could not escape from it and sure enough a few days later, just after we had spoken about MacLeod for the first time, I received a visitor in my apartment. It was Captain Stein. I was shocked and angered by his appearance. I took him inside hoping no one had seen him enter my chambers. I was livid that he would visit me so soon after the discovery of MacLeod's body and by doing so establish a link between the two of us. Stein told me he had visited MacLeod's lodgings and removed a commonplace book and some other documents of interest to him. In his hand, he held MacLeod's paper outlining the allegations against my daughter. Stein said he was impressed by MacLeod's careful book keeping of his illicit practices. He would learn from this, he said, and apply it to the business of extortion. He said he would get straight to the point. He cursed Gourlay and his gang and said he would soon rule the town instead of them. He needed men like me on his side. Gourlay would soon be finished. He knew Gourlay had tried to kill him in the Canongate explosion. He would have his revenge soon enough. I was stunned by his next proposal. He told me I was to become his man. I was to work for him. I was to advise him on legal matters. I was to be employed by scum like him. I tasted bile when I heard this. There was worse. For his silence on matters relating to my daughter, I was to pay him a quarterly sum, or he would go to Dewarton. When I heard this, I was speechless. Pain suffused my chest and ran down my arm. I found myself short of breath. I collapsed unable to gather my thoughts. I realised I was surely undone. I had sinned against God and God was punishing me. He had sent Satan to accost me. I was caught in a web of evil. I had chosen a path from which there was no escape. I had transferred one blackmailer for another and the new one was much deadlier. You can imagine how I felt the next day when Gourlay's headless corpse was found and the name Stein was on everyone's lips as the new power in town. He also made hints that if I refused his offer, the lives of my wife and daughter were in danger.

The news about Killiecrankie reached the city that night. The place was in mayhem. It stimulated me to act. I was excited by the hope that Presbyterian rule might soon be over. I paced about my chambers for hours, pondering different courses of action. Finally, I decided on one. Once I had made my decision, I felt calmness descend on me for the first time in weeks. I met Stein again and told him I would agree to his terms. I would meet him the following day in my chambers to make the first payment. I would help him run the town and other such flattery. I did not sleep that night. I was haunted by a myriad of ghosts from the past, but in the cold light of day I was resolved upon what I should do. That was last night, John. My last night in this world.

This is what I resolved to do, John. I would hide a loaded pistol under my coat. I would meet Stein at the appointed hour and take him back to my chambers, sending my man back to Tyneford House. I wanted everyone to see us together. The thing had gone too far. I was a lost man, forsaken. It was time to restore my dignity, to restore some control over my life. I remembered Stein's grin as he read the accusations, surely only to torture me, as he stood at the window in my chamber. I will not hesitate. I will stand a few feet from him. A calmness will descend over me. I will say something like: 'I have your first payment, Mr Stein. It's the payment of a gentleman to a turd!' I will pull out my pistol and shoot him in the face, rejoicing as his head is blown off, spraying blood and brain across the wall. He will collapse on the floor. I will take my other pistol and shoot him through the heart as he lies beneath me to make sure he is no more.

I have cast all the documents to the flames. I ask only that you oversee my legal affairs and look after the interest of my wife and daughter. Only you know the truth of the matter and my sin of murder and self-murder. I have engineered it so it will be presented differently. It will look like there has been a struggle in my chamber with the killer of Gourlay. We exchanged fire. Both of us are no more. I ask you, as a true friend, to preserve my reputation and ensure my daughter receives the wedding she deserves. Finally, please arrange the publication of my book at some point in the future. You have complete editorial authority to do with it as you think fit. I have completed it at last. Perhaps, I understand finally how a land at peace may fall into the awful pit of civil strife. Evil walks in this land, John. Evil is deep within the heart of man. Evil is unleashed by revolution against established authority. God save King James.

Your friend and fellow traveller,
Archibald Stirling

Epilogue

SCOUGALL SAT IN the Royal Coffee House taking his morning cup alone. A second meeting with Chrissy Munro had gone well. They had walked together along the shore at Musselburgh. She had taken his arm. He was certainly taken with her. She was pretty and clever and bubbled with life. He wondered if she liked him. She had come back a second time, but was it just to please her parents? His mother was delighted. It was already agreed they should meet for a third time. Then he would ask her, and if she hinted she was inclined to accept, he would go to her father to ask permission. He was sure she was the one for him. His life was about to change fundamentally. He would have to leave Mrs Baird's lodgings and take rooms somewhere else in the city as a married man. He might think about a small property near Musselburgh, his own retreat in the country. He was as happy as he had been in a long time, despite the terrible end of Stirling. He pictured himself on Musselburgh Links, playing a round of golf with his own son.

A boy was wandering from table to table, distributing copies of the *Gazette*. Scougall purchased one and sat back contentedly to read it. He took a sip of coffee and began to read a piece describing the marriage of Dewarton's son to Arabella Stirling in a small ceremony at Dewarton House. It mentioned how her father was recently slain in tragic circumstances defending himself from Captain Andrew Stein, the murderer of George Gourlay, the respected tavern-owner. It was a small ceremony because she was still in mourning for her beloved father.

Scougall felt himself well-up with emotion. The world would never know the truth. Stirling's turmoil and his role in killing MacLeod. It was unjust for MacLeod's kin, but it was better that way. MacKenzie had told MacLeod's father that Stein was the killer, which was, after all, true. MacLeod's body was embalmed and taken back for burial in Harris.

His eyes moved down to another article. It was about the aftermath of Killiecrankie. The Jacobite army had not reached the south as feared but fragmented following the victory as Highland armies usually did. Dundee was killed on the battlefield and his troops left rudderless. Scougall read the subtitle: A list of dead at the battle of Killiecrankie which occurred on the 27th July 1689. The Jacobites slain in the battle were listed on one side of the page and on the other those on the government side. His eyes scanned the lists, looking for names he recognised. Dundee was at the top of the Jacobite side. Then a name threw him completely. He felt himself fall for a moment. It was so unexpected. Ruairidh MacKenzie, Seaforth's brother, had fallen at Killiecrankie. A sudden feeling of elation rushed through him. Elizabeth was free of the foolish Papist. He knew she would be heart-broken but he could not help rejoicing. God forgive him. God forgive him. He should not rejoice the death of any man. He closed his eyes and opened his soul to his Maker. Forgive me such thoughts, oh Lord, forgive me. Oh, Lord forgive me. But let her return safely. Let her return. Let her return safely. He prayed with all his heart.

Luath Press Limited

committed to publishing well written books worth reading

LUATH PRESS takes its name from Robert Burns, whose little collie Luath (*Gael.*, swift or nimble) tripped up Jean Armour at a wedding and gave him the chance to speak to the woman who was to be his wife and the abiding love of his life. Burns called one of the 'Twa Dogs' Luath after Cuchullin's hunting dog in Ossian's *Fingal*. Luath Press was established in 1981 in the heart of Burns country, and is now based a few steps up the road from Burns' first lodgings on Edinburgh's Royal Mile. Luath offers you distinctive writing with a hint of unexpected pleasures.

Most bookshops in the UK, the US, Canada, Australia, New Zealand and parts of Europe, either carry our books in stock or can order them for you. To order direct from us, please send a £sterling cheque, postal order, international money order or your credit card details (number, address of cardholder and expiry date) to us at the address below. Please add post and packing as follows: UK – £1.00 per delivery address; overseas surface mail – £2.50 per delivery address; overseas airmail – £3.50 for the first book to each delivery address, plus £1.00 for each additional book by airmail to the same address. If your order is a gift, we will happily enclose your card or message at no extra charge.

Luath Press Limited
543/2 Castlehill
The Royal Mile
Edinburgh EH1 2ND
Scotland
Telephone: +44 (0)131 225 4326 (24 hours)
email: sales@luath. co.uk
Website: www. luath.co.uk